Perilous Passage

A Boots Beaumont Mystery

By Joe Soll

"Perilous Passage"
By Joe Soll

ISBN: 978-0-692-24021-2

Library of Congress Cataloging-in-Publication Data
Soll, Joe (date)

Includes bibliographical references.

Dedication: To the memory of Ruth Braverman

Acknowledgements:

I would like to thank CM and Alexsandra for their proofreading skills and excellent editing suggestions; the late John D. MacDonald whose works inspired the character of Boots Beaumont.

Special thanks to Lori Paris for her help in the creation of the fictional characters of Boots, Cappy, Julie and Yvonne.

Previous Boot's Beaumont mysteries…

By Joe Soll & Lori Paris

1 Evil Exchange 2007
2 Fatal Flight   2010

Also by Joe Soll

I Almost Fell of the Top of the Empire State Building   2014

Adoption Healing... a path to recovery (for adoptees) 2000
Adoption Healing... a path to recovery Supplement   2011
Adoption Healing... a path to recovery Articles, Etc.   2013

with Karen Wilson Buterbaugh as co-author,
Adoption Healing (For women who lost children to adoption)
2003

입양 치유.. 입양으로 아이를 잃은 어머니의 회복과 성숙을 위한
카운슬링 **2013** *Adoption Healing* (*For women who lost children to adoption)* in Korean

Heilungsprozess für Adoptierte ... Ein Weg zur Verarbeitung 2014
Übersetzt Cornelia Nietzschmann geb. Rösler
with Conny Nietzschmann, *Adoption Healing* in German

Prologue – *From the Eagle Chronicles*

A sliver of autumn moonlight in a gauzy sky shone on the transom of the "Serendipity" as she lay at anchor. The boat rocked gently in Princess Bay, a cove on the north side of Hurricane Hole at the east end of St. John in the U.S. Virgin Islands. The only sound was the lapping water against the stern of the boat as Falcon's head lifted slowly out of the dark depths, the eagle's eye tattoo on his neck glistened and seemed to wink it's okay as he waited, listening for any sound from the boat.

He had left the mini-sub through the airlock only a few minutes ago and swam straight up, holding his breath until he reached the surface where he now reviewed the 55' Wheeler in his mind. With a little online research, he knew the cabin layout by heart. Clad in a black wetsuit, he was nearly invisible. The wetsuit felt itchy on his skin. It wasn't for warmth as the sea here was never cold enough to need one. The suit would serve another purpose soon enough. He wiped the salt water from his lips and smiled.

The young couple would be in the master stateroom forward of the wheelhouse and he wanted to be sure they were asleep before he climbed all the way aboard. At two in the morning he presumed they would be asleep, but he wanted to be sure. Patience was key in his line of work. That, and the element of surprise. He and the others had been cruising the shoreline in Hurricane Hole from 1000 yards out when they had seen the young couple swimming alongside the boat and watched them for a full day to be sure they were alone on board.

After some time, Falcon crawled slowly over the stern, sat on the built-in transom seat, took the waterproof pouch from around his waist, opened it and removed the stun gun. He left the pouch on the cushion before moving forward. He grabbed the salon door and turned it careful to not make any noise. Good thing it's not locked. He could pick a lock of course, was very good at it in fact, but locks can take time and make noise. He went forward to the open stateroom door. He could make out two figures lying in bed. He went to the left side where the larger figure lay and quickly shoved the stun gun to an exposed neck. "Zzzzzzzzzzzap." The body jerked and was still, but the gun caused a racket, no doubt. The person on the other side of the bed screamed, jumped up, and ran into the salon. Falcon could see a flimsy night-gowned figure and rushed after her. Christ, this one's fast. "But," he thought, "no one is faster than the Falcon." Falcon made a leap not unlike a ballet move and grabbed one slender ankle with his left hand while pressing the stun gun to her thigh as she fell. She was out for the count.

Better get to it. He jogged back to the stern and removed a knife, small tarp, and a battery operated Sawzall out of the pouch. He couldn't help but grin.

He spread the tarp out by the woman, picked her up as if she weighed nothing and dropped her back down. She moaned as he bent down and quickly shoved the knife into her heart. Her body struggled a bit, but it didn't take long. Before he began his wet work, Falcon returned to the salon and gave the unconscious man another jolt until it was his turn. Now the fun begins, but where to start? He took the Sawzall and thought for a moment before going to her lower extremities. The saw was efficient for its size, but it took time. After the second leg was detached, he straightened up, threw the legs overboard, and went back to work. He was careful to keep the tarp raised to prevent blood spatter on the boat itself, but it was messy work. He went to work on the arms, then severed the head and set it off to the side in the bait well of the boat.

"Might as well watch, sweet cheeks,' he told her. He threw the rest of her body overboard and went to the salon to get the man.

The guy was heavier of course, but not too heavy to bring aft to the tarp. Falcon wasn't a large man but he was strong. "Brute strength. Fucking brute strength, that's what I got," he'd like to boast. As he carried his unconscious captive, the man's head bumped the overhead. "Aw, did that hurt you? Hey, not to worry, we'll fix you up in a bit. No more pain ever. I promise," he said and he patted the man on the back. The Sawzall buzzed as Falcon severed the man's limbs and then the head from the trunk of his body. He set the man's head in the bait well facing the woman's and threw the torso overboard as well.

"The sharks will be so happy to see you kids." He expertly whistled "Taps" as he threw both heads to the sea in final farewell.

Falcon rolled up the tarp and tied it with a small piece of rope, then threw it over the stern, knowing the sharks would smell the blood and tear it to shreds. He removed the walkie-talkie from the pouch and keyed the switch. When he heard the answering click he said, "Falcon here, score is two zip," and released the switch. He leaned over the transom and pasted on the large self-stick plastic sheet that proclaimed the boat to be *Hornby* and disappearing *Serendipity* forever.

Humming to himself, he went straight to the head and turned on the hot water. When steam indicated the correct temperature, he stepped in. He let the water rinse the wetsuit then rinsed it off and scrubbed himself from head to toe. "Have to be clean. Have to be clean. Be clean or else." The familiar chant rang in his head. Twenty minutes later, wearing a fresh towel like a kilt, he turned on the bilge fans, and after a few minutes started the engines and warmed up the sonar. The image of the mini-sub started to move southeast and he followed. He thought of the couple on their way to the depths. What a waste of good meat. I wish I had had time to eat.

Chapter One

Day eight of the new year was much like the seven before it. Brilliant blue sky, a mild breeze, and the ocean was calm. The high would reach 75° and no rain was forecast for the next twenty-four hours. Most of the tourists had reluctantly left the Bahamian island of Eleuthera to return home to exchange bathing suits and sarongs for thermal underwear and parkas. Relishing the quiet, my two friends and I lounged comfortably on a condo balcony in Cupid's Cay, overlooking the marina, just north of Governor's Harbor on the west side of the island where Pine Street meets Queen's Highway. We were sipping Bloody Marys and watching the harbor regain its leisurely non-touristy pace. I could just make out my *Lost & Found* tied up at the marina's outermost pier.

We acknowledged what a relief it was to have the holidays behind us as it really wasn't our favorite time of the year, for a number of different reasons. We did however thoroughly enjoy New Year's Eve, and we were rehashing the wedding we'd attended. We agreed it was one of the best we'd ever been to. Bebe and Winston were a beautiful and fun loving couple and absolutely crazy about each other. Their simple ceremony held on the beach after sunset with Tiki torches providing the glow and tropical flowers scenting the air went without a hitch. The bride was a vision, her groom beaming with pride. The minister had all in attendance laughing with marital anecdotes and crying with the memory of loved ones no longer here on earth but surely looking down from high above. All in all, it was an elegant, refined, sophisticated, and stylish event. That was until the reception, and then all hell broke loose.

Suddenly, I laughed so hard I couldn't catch my breath. My face was crimson and tears squirted from my eyes. Yvonne bopped me a good one on the shoulder to try and get me to stop. No luck. Ever the diplomat, Yvonne did her absolute best not to become an accomplice, but she could only hold out for so long. A stifled squeal broke through, and seconds later, even the primary target, Cappy, began to giggle.

"What? I am a good dancer, better than you Boots Beaumont. You just haven't seen moves like that before," Cappy said in his defense.

"You're right. I haven't seen moves like that. Ever. And I hope I never do again." I'd finally taken a breath and found my voice. "Cap, you do a mean version of the worm, you know that? How'd you even know about it anyway?"

"Must've seen it online somewhere, I guess. YouTube most likely."

"I didn't know you had it in you." I said as I wiped my eyes.

"I had jello shots in me, that's what I had," said Cappy as he winced at the memory. "Those things sneak up on you, damn."

"Vonnie liked them too," I grinned. "You led the conga line, didn't you, babe?"

An expert at changing the subject, Yvonne answered right back. "And look who's speaking? 'Mr. Kara-dopey' I believe that's what they called you. You sang a Jimmy Buffet song, didn't you?" She scrunched her face in distaste.

"Thank God Julie took the mic away from you before you could embarrass yourself any further," Cappy added.

A brief, but awkward moment followed. Julie D'Arville and I had been engaged ourselves in the not so distant past. If our relationship had been complicated, our split had been even more so, but it simply boiled down to two people wanting two different things. While Julie and I were busy trying to straighten out the mess we were in, Yvonne Franzen was literally thrown into the mix when I pulled her out of the water after a plane crash that we witnessed. Julie ended up leaving, Yvonne ended up staying. But even after almost a year, not everyone had moved on, at least not all the way, and it was evident at the wedding.

Yvonne directed the conversation back to the bride and groom. "When are they due back from their honeymoon anyway?"

"Yesterday, I do believe. The sign on Winston's dive shop said it would reopen today. Must have decided to stay out a bit longer," Cappy said nonchalantly. Island time ran at its own pace and most everyone who lived there preferred it that way.

"That's not really like him though," I commented with a frown. "He loves that shop. He wouldn't even let anyone else keep it open for him while they were gone, even for a month's honeymoon."

"I'm sure there's nothing to worry about. They probably can't pry themselves away from each other. I'm sure we'll see them today or tomorrow." Cappy drained his glass and jiggled the ice cubes. "Another round?"

From the Eagle Chronicles # 1

Eagle was relaxing in the shade of the fantail of *Raptor*, his 64' Krogen Expedition. He was moored in the northwestern most corner of Cowpet Bay in the fashionable East End of St. Thomas in the U.S. Virgin Islands. He'd gotten the coded message from Buzzard on the mini-sub. It was on his Blackberry when he woke up a few hours earlier. "Falcon here, score is two zip," followed by the numbers, 03911211 8133015 3144681.

He had written the numbers down on a notepad, circling the sixth and seventh number of each set. 11/15/81 was Buzzard's birthday which meant that she was not forced to send the message. He eliminated the circled numbers and wrote the rest of the numbers backwards starting with the seventh and fifteenth numbers which gave him 1821193064413033 which he then punctuated to 18°21'19.30 north longitude, 64°41'30.33 west latitude. He went to his computer, loaded Google Earth, and punched in the coordinates which brought him to Princess Bay, about 15 miles from Cowpet Bay. Allowing for the prevailing winds, traveling at 4 knots or roughly 4.6 miles per hour, it would be about four hours before Buzzard and Falcon arrived with his newest acquisition.

Martha, the silly young one he "rescued" a few days ago from an overturned sunfish while he was out in his Zodiac was on board with him. She'd just wandered into his cove where a wave from a passing ferry had swamped her. He went right to her and pulled her out of the water and into his "Z" runabout. "Want to come aboard and dry off with a bit of rum to take away the shakes?" He'd asked with a toothy grin. She'd readily agreed, and he figured it was partly because she was shaking, partly because she could see he was ruggedly handsome, and partly because *Raptor* was one beautiful hunk of yacht. They weren't visible to anyone outside of the cove so he wasn't worried about her being seen with him. He'd rescued her just before dusk last night and she seemed quite content to stick around. While she got into some dry clothes he gave her, clothes from ladies past, he used the zodiac to go back to her sunfish, right it, furl the sail and tie it to the stern of his boat. He'd decide what to do with it later. Probably set it adrift with full sail... it would go southeast with the prevailing breeze and then just drift. It would be one of the mysteries of the sea. Martha wanted adventure and she'd found it. He casually asked her enough questions to know that she was alone on vacation, had come down to St. Thomas on a whim from Lino Lakes, Minnesota, and had told no one where she was going. A perfect situation. Too bad. I'll have to get rid of her before Buzzard and Falcon get back. Too bad because she's very cute, but Buzzard would go bonkers if she caught me. Nevertheless, we have a few days to have fun. Martha's down in the galley making lunch and after that . . . His thoughts were interrupted by Martha calling him. "On my way, honey." he answered in anticipated delight.

While they were enjoying the lunch Martha prepared, tuna mixed with slivered almonds and served on a bed of Belgian endive, his thoughts wandered back to the beginning.

Stephen Danker had grown up on Salt Spring Island in British Columbia. Tempered by the prevailing westerly winds, warm enough for palm trees to flourish, SSI as it was referred to, was a wonderful place to grow up, for most people that is. But with an alcoholic mother and a rageaholic, sadistic father, Stephen's childhood was hell. He was regularly beaten for no particular reason, and often left unfed. Not unfed because of a lack of money, but rather unfed because his mother was out drinking and his father was out trying to gamble away the family fortune which was vast. A fortune of which Stephen was unaware. Stephen learned how to fend for himself and often stayed with the families of his school friends. When he was in his teens, he heard about nearby Hornby Island, a refuge for eagles. He and a skiff-owning friend of his motored to the island to look around. They tied the boat to a stump that was embedded in the shore and went for a walk. As they were walking, they heard a high-pitched screeching and turning to follow the sound, they saw an eagle, talons extended, swoop down and pull a salmon from the water. As the eagle flew off to enjoy its meal, Stephan had a stark realization. Some day, I'll be like that eagle and just take what I want. Stephen and his friend explored the island, and found a plaque on a 120' tall tree. The plaque stated that there was an eagle's nest near the top of the tree with hidden cameras to observe the eagles' activities. There was a website listed which Stephen noted in his memory bank.

Later at home, Stephen used the family computer to look at the eagles' nest. He saw two eagles working on a nest, preparing it for the laying of eggs. He had to be careful using the computer so he wouldn't get a beating, but he was good at being a sneak. He had had to learn that to survive in his home. Whenever he could, he was on line studying raptors. He learned that there were five birds classified as raptors: buzzard, eagle, falcon, hawk and owl.

He decided that if he could be any animal he wanted, he'd be an eagle. I'd fly anywhere I wished and take whatever I wanted, whenever I wanted it. I'd be invincible, he thought to himself.

"Hey."

"Huh?"

"Eagle, are you listening to me?" asked Martha.

"Sure, Martha, sure," he replied. He had no idea what she'd been saying.

"Good. Let's do it."

"Do what?" Eagle asked.

"Go below and have fun, silly. You said yes, didn't you?"

"I sure did, my little chick. I sure did."

Chapter Two

"Another trip? But you just got back a month ago," I said. To my embarrassment, I knew I sounded petulant. I couldn't remember ever sounding that way in my life, even as a kid. I could barely believe it was possible.

"But I've always wanted to go to Croatia, there is a famous national park there where the waterfalls are so beautiful," Yvonne began.

"It's cold there now, isn't it?" I said. "You want to go during the winter?"

"Less tourists, Boots" she answered and shrugged her shoulders.

"Right. Whatever," I groused and went back to unpacking groceries in the galley of my beloved 63' Cheoy Lee motorsailer, the Lost & Found which I'd inherited from my Uncle Sammy whom I had never met. Yvonne was clearly hurt by my curt attitude. She hesitated, looked as if she were going to give up, and then changed her mind.

"Why don't you come with me?" She stepped close to me and reached out, taking my hand in hers.

"Vonnie, come on. We've talked about this before," I answered and then sighed. "I can't just take off all the time, my editor is breathing down my neck, and the old gal here needs some maintenance . . ." I knew it sounded lame. I also knew it didn't really matter if I went or not. It wasn't about that at all.

Almost since Yvonne Frazen came in to my life, it seemed she wanted to leave it. The story of how we met isn't a romantic one in the slightest, it is a story that you would only pass on to your grandchildren if you wanted them to have nightmares. Yvonne had been the sole survivor of a plane crash and I, the Johnny on the drink, but that was only the beginning. She lost her lover in the crash, lost her roommate to a psychopath, fell in love with me, survived a sniper attack and was almost killed by a scorned woman.

Interestingly enough, she had no fear of flying, even right after the crash, but she seemed terrified of getting too close to anyone. As soon as she and I tried to settle into some kind of routine, her nerves would get the better of her and she'd vanish. Eventually, she would return. We would talk. She tried to explain her feelings. I tried to understand, to put myself in her shoes. We'd go on for a bit and then the cycle would repeat. At some point, and quite separately, we both turned to Cappy for help.

Vincente Ciacci, or Cappy was a therapist from New York. He and I were longtime friends, and when I left the city for the island, Cappy realized life was short, his savings account was big, and the move was, as some might say, a "no-brainer." Cappy was one of the first to speak to Yvonne after her tragic accident, and she quickly developed a deep trust in the unassuming man. He'd even hypnotized her now and then to help ease the anxiety she suffered. Over time, he counseled her sporadically, but only when she asked. He explained survivor's guilt over and over. Intellectually, she understood, she got it. Survivors are prone to depression, social withdrawal, sleep issues, have difficulty getting along with others, and possess a tremendous fear of being out of control. But emotionally, all she could feel was a looming sense that any happiness she achieved would surely be taken away. Her reaction was to flee.

At first, Yvonne would return to Florida, where she'd lived and worked for many years. A flight attendant for Transcon Airlines, she'd been involved with a pilot who happened to be married with two kids. Captain Wellman perished in the plane crash, and some months later, it was revealed that his life insurance policy named Yvonne as the only beneficiary. Yvonne received a rather large sum of money, which she then used to fund her "trips" as she called them. She stopped going to Florida and set her sights on more distant locations. I knew what these "trips" really were, an excuse. A way to legitimately disappear for a while, based on her "love" of travel. I didn't doubt that she had a travel bug, many people are flight attendants for that very reason. Yvonne was Dutch, she still had family there, distant cousins or something. She went to visit a few times, then seemed determined to travel to as many European countries as she could. I had joined her once or twice, and we'd shared some good experiences together, but I preferred my life on Eleuthera. The weather was warm, the pace was slow, I had good friends, a quiet place to write the mystery novels I was so well known for after retiring, and, I was content. Besides, what Yvonne was doing wasn't exploring, it was escaping. It was painfully obvious to me that she was trying to find herself, while insisting she was trying to educate herself.

Although it wasn't easy for me to talk about my feelings, I did try a time or two with Cappy. The advice I got was to be patient, to be sensitive and aware of Yvonne's fragile state after going through as much as she did. Patience and sensitivity were words mostly absent from my vocabulary. I'd been a cop turned private investigator until a sniper's bullet lodged itself in my skull. I didn't retire early only because of the bullet, but because I'd had enough of the dark side of life and the winter weather caused enough pain from said bullet to remind me on a daily basis that I was far more likely to get shot living in a big city than on a small island.

When Julie and I met on Eleuthera, our relationship was volatile, passionate, unpredictable, and complicated. Julie never expected me to be sweet or nurturing or thoughtful. Yes, we loved each other, but we were bonded by physical attraction, sex, lust, desire, and best of all, make-up sex, which was frequent considering how often we fought. Our eventual break-up was difficult. And when I became involved with Yvonne, I really wanted to make a go of it. I was over fifty, and while I didn't think of myself in the conventional light with a wife and kids, I did want to take a stab at a permanent union with the right person. I'd been doing my best over the last year. I quit swearing, was more polite, did my utmost to tame my unruly ego, and I really tried to listen and empathize. I felt I'd made a lot of progress and was damn proud of it, which is why I just didn't understand things weren't going better.

"Knock, knock," Cappy called out.

"Hey, you old pirate. Come aboard," I called back. I was relieved that Vonnie and I were interrupted.

"Well, I come with disconcerting news," Cappy entered the galley and squeezed himself between us.

"Really, what should it be?" Yvonne asked.

"What could it be," Cappy absentmindedly corrected. Yvonne still mixed up English phrases and words though she'd been in the states for many years.

"Well, out with it," I prompted.

"No word from Bebe and Winston. They're a week overdue," Cappy reported with a frown.

"Aw, c'mon Cap, that's no big deal, they just probably decided to stay longer . . ."

"No, Boots. It's more than that. No one can reach them. There's been no radio contact for days. Winston's employees are really concerned. He would never let the business be closed for so long," Cappy said.

"Has the Coast Guard been called?" I said.

"Yes. Winston's assistant manager at the dive shop, Edward, called them today. They've sent out a patrol and some others have gone out on their own to help look." Cappy always knew the island gossip since he played backgammon with various locals.

"I hope they are okay," Yvonne said and then shivered. She didn't like any talk of bad news.

"Let's not jump to conclusions, babe. I'm sure they're all right," I assured her. I put an arm around her for a quick hug. But I didn't believe it myself, not for one minute. I felt something was wrong. The ocean was a dangerous place and I had learned to trust my guts..

"Hey Cappy, do you want to go the market with me?" asked Yvonne.

"Sure, anything for you, Yvonne," said Cappy giving me a wink and they went out the aft door of the salon.

I went forward from the salon and down a few steps into my starboard side office which was just behind the forward stateroom and across from the leeward side quarters. I checked my email and found had none. I was frustrated and just not understanding what was going on with Yvonne. I sat there looking out the window at the long dock that led back to the marina office. We were tied up at the end of a "T" pier, broadside to the "T" because of the length of the boat. I could see Cappy's terrace on the hill that rose above and south of the marina. I heard the comforting sounds of seagulls and water lapping at the side of the boat. I heard a jet coming in for a landing at the airport just to the north of us and wondered where they would be going. There would be vacationers, newly-weds, old marrieds and perhaps potential investors thinking of putting up one more vacation village here on what I have come to look at as my island. *My island and I didn't want any more tourists than we already had.* I wonder why I had a thought like that. The tourists don't bother me at all.

From the Eagle Chronicles # 2

"Passing Ram Head. 3 hours out. Buzzard with Falcon tailing. Out." Eagle closed the flap on his cell phone. Hopefully they won't call for another few hours. Martha and I won't have any interruptions. He smiled knowing all was on schedule and that hopefully Buzzard would not be calling at an inopportune moment. Martha may have been a ditz, but she was a most willing partner. She had a few moves (not to mention the tongue ring) that kept him interested. More than interested, he could barely keep his hands off her. "Who was that?" asked Martha.

God, she asks a lot of questions, but she's supremely good in the sack. Too bad I have only a few more days before she has to be turned off.

They were lying in bed relaxing after another bout of screamingly good sex. To say that Martha tended to vocalize her feelings was a bit of an understatement. Not that he minded, not at all. Eagle thought healthy expressions of enjoyment only heightened the experience, but he was glad she wouldn't be around much longer. People loved to gossip, especially when it came to beautiful women aboard yachts. He was always discreet, but if word every got back to Buzzard, he'd be instant road kill, and she would happily rip his heart right out of his chest and eat it. The thought of eating made his stomach rumble a bit. He wished he could sail over to Bonnie's-By-The-Sea for lunch, but he simply could not afford to be seen with the wanna-be porno star.

"Just some friends, no worries," he said and nuzzled her neck.

"Do all your friends have bird names?"

"It's just a game we play," he said softly and changed the subject. "How about making us some lunch?"

"Sure, I'm hungry.   How about I fry up some conch from yesterday's haul?"

"Sounds good," Eagle gave her a friendly booty swat as she hopped out of bed.

He threw on some clothes and went out on deck. He was surprised to see dark gray clouds that hovered just above his head. The air was still and heavy and smelled of tin. As soon as he felt the first light drops of rain, he returned indoors. Eagle didn't care much for the rain, even warm tropical rain. It made him grouchy. He forgot about his hunger and decided to hide out for a bit in the office. He knew it would be a while before he ate, Martha's skills did not lie in the culinary arena.

His thoughts returned to the "game" he'd casually mentioned after Martha asked about the phone call. He sat down at his desk, put his feet up on the cool mahogany surface while scrunching down in the luxurious leather swivel chair. Reflecting on the past, he remembered that what had started innocently enough eventually turned into a deadly game. And a very profitable one at that.

He had watched, along with several thousand others around the world, as the female eagle laid two eggs in the nest on Hornby Island. One of the two eggs hatched and Doug, the Island's Eagle Master, had named it Phoenix. He'd watched Phoenix grow, day by day, watched the feathers appear, watched the mother eagle hover over her baby during storms, feed him constantly with pieces of fish torn off the carcasses of those she caught and brought to the nest. He watched, as eagle lovers around the world watched, when inexplicably, Phonenix started to gasp for breath and died. He cried, sobbed as he never had before, and vowed to never get attached to anything or anyone again. He vowed to get even with the Gods for taking Phoenix from him. He took it as personally as he did when his parents disappeared without a word when he was seventeen. Their whereabouts were never discovered. He had to work as a mate on the private yachts of Salt Springs' residents to survive. He was a hard worker, but as he loved the water, he felt natural at sea and soon learned navigation and how to sail. He made enough money to rent a small apartment on the island, get a computer, date a few women, and have some fun. Eagle had a knack for playing poker and consistently won to the consternation of the locals. He could read people's faces, even poker faces. He was good enough to have won and saved over forty thousand dollars in a period of five years.

At age twenty-four, he'd been able to land a job as captain for a rich, old couple who owned a 40' ketch. They'd returned from a week long voyage to nowhere and he was hosing off the decks when a dapper gentleman in a three-piece suit called out to him. "Are you Stephen Danker?"

"You are?"

"An attorney and I need to find Stephen Danker. Is that you?"

He held his breath, "Yes and?"

"Where can we talk in private, Mr. Danker?"

"I guess up here. Come on up the gang plank."

The lawyer came on board and Stephen leaned against the stern railing, body tensed to react in case of danger though he did not sense a threat. "What's this about?"

"My name is Stuart Mitcher. I am a probate attorney for the province of British Columbia. Seven years ago your parents disappeared. Since there has been no trace of them they are now presumed dead. You, being their only heir, are to receive their assets which are considerable."

"Considerable? We lived like paupers. I'm afraid you have the wrong Stephen Danker."

"No, we've checked into this very carefully. The estate, valued at seven million four hundred thousand Canadian dollars is now yours."

"Seven what?" asked Stephen incredulously as he gripped the railing to keep himself under control.

"Seven million four hundred thousand Canadian dollars, sir. The funds are in the Bank of Canada under your name. All you need is your driver's license and birth certificate to have access to the money."

"I'm speechless, Mr. Mitcher."

"I would be too, Mr. Danker. Good luck and good day to you."

The attorney turned, went down the gangplank and briskly walked towards the parking lot.

Stephen Danker went into the salon and roared with laughter.

Now he was truly free to exact his revenge.

One day, while surfing the web looking for pictures of eagles he came across the mention of a new Facebook group called "Raptor Lovers." He hadn't watched the Hornby Island eagle webcam since the death of Phoenix, and realized how much he missed the connection, even though this was something different. He joined the Facebook group. There were a half dozen other raptor obsessives in the group, some using their real first names and a few with names of raptors… Buzzard, Falcon, Hawk, and Owl. He quickly took the name of Eagle and joined in the postings. They all had watched the death of Phoenix and it became a topic of conversation for a few days until they started to talk about themselves. No first names were ever shared. Little by little, they opened up to one another through private messages. Much later he found out that Buzzard, the only woman, was a stripper who lived in Scranton. Hawk was a naval architect living in Tampa, Falcon was a pharmacist in Dayton, and Owl was professor of literature at UCLA. Though their stories varied, the common thread was a general disillusionment with relationships, a hatred of big government, the inequality of rich and poor, freedom versus constraints, and crappy childhoods.

Eagle's mind began to soar with possibilities. A plan to have fun and get richer at the expense of others who had had what he deserved. He needed accomplices and he suspected that his new raptor family might be the answer. How to probe deeper without tipping his hand was the first challenge, but he sensed this could be the beginning of a new and wonderful life.

Chapter Three

My Heineken was getting warm so I gulped down the last of it and decided I was lazy enough to not want to get up and into the shade of the cabin, even though the Caribbean sun was fierce this 13th of February. I like the number 13, it's always been good to me, except on lotto tickets where it never seems to matter what combinations of 13 I use... Maybe I should stop playing.

Yvonne was still not back from the market in North Eleuthera where she was getting some much needed groceries. Cappy went with her as he wanted to just expand his horizons, whatever that meant given this small town on this tiny island.

I was having some fantasies about what Vonnie and I could be doing later, after Cappy left, when the phone rang. The caller ID said it was Julie, calling from New York. Sometimes I think she knows just when to interrupt my thoughts.. Good grief, I need to watch my own thinking about her thinking. Perhaps I should discuss it with Cappy.

"Hey Jules, how are you?"

"Boots, can you talk? she said rapidly.

"Sure, what's up?" I said as I got up and walked to the window of the main cabin, catching my reflection on the glass. All bronzed 6' 1" of me, Boots Beaumont, ex-PI, ex-mystery writer, practicing neither, dabbling in both.

"Boots, have you heard from Bebe and Winston?"

"No, Jules, I haven't, I know they are more than a week overdue and we are all concerned." I know she knows something or she wouldn't have called.

"I just know something is wrong, Boots. You know sometimes, I just know things. She is my niece and I just know she would have called if they were going to stay longer."

"Jules, do you know their itinerary? What islands they were going to sail to?"

"As I recall, they had chartered a 37' Tayana ketch from the Hatchet Bay Marina and had filed a navigation plan with their office. Boots, please look into it, please?"

"Julie, I'll get on it right away. Do you have any special thoughts about what is wrong?"

"Not exactly. I just see trouble, Boots. I see vague shadows, nothing more than that. By the way, how are you and... Never mind. Keep me posted, please."

"I will, I.. " There was a click at the other end as she hung up abruptly. I think she was going to ask about Yvonne and decided it was a bad idea and she was right.

I left a note for Cappy and Vonnie, put on some sandals and walked down the dock to the parking lot to my old war-surplus jeep. I had put on cut-offs and an old Club Med T-shirt when I woke up and I figured that was good enough, so I headed over to the police department in Governor's Harbor.

Dust swirled as I drove over the unpaved rode into downtown Governor's Harbor. I passed abandoned cars, ramshackle houses and children playing in back yards. As I got closer to town, the road became paved and the houses in better repair. I passed a gas station and saw the grocery store. The police department office was across the street from the grocery store, on the ground floor of a pastel blue, two story clapboard building that had seen better days. Being on Queen's Highway forgave some of the antiquity. I walked in and approached the desk where a policeman sat reading a newspaper. A ceiling fan moved the hot air around the room as I waited. After what seemed like minutes, he looked up and said, "Yes?" with a look of hostility, perhaps because I interrupted his reading.

"Is Lieutenant Thomas Greenslade around?" I said"

He stiffened and said, "Who is asking, sir?"

All of a sudden I rated a "sir" because I asked for his boss by name. "Boots Beaumont, an old friend of his."

"One moment, sir" and he picked up the phone and murmured into it. "He'll be right down, sir, please have a seat."

"Thank you, officer." I sat down and looked around the room. I'd not been in here for over a year and I could see that it was freshly painted in a lime green with Bahamian travel posters proclaiming, "It's better in the Bahamas" and BahamasAir advertisements on the wall.

"Boots, how are you?" boomed Thomas Greenslade, as he appeared in a doorway at the back of the room, motioning me to come and join him. Magically, the newspaper in the officer's hand had become a police department procedural manual.

I walked back and into his office which was, while not luxurious, had the warmth of a den in a country home... plaques and certificates of accomplishment, photos of Tom with smiling dignitaries, a dozen trophies and an old oak desk.

We shook hands and I sat down in front of his desk as he closed the door to his office. We'd met during the investigation of the plane crash, the one that Yvonne had survived, and become fast friends. Tom was a native Eleutheran with a BS in Criminal Justice from the University of Miami. Although his police department was not a very busy one, during the tourist season there could be a lot of activity requiring his undivided attention. The powers-that-be did not want anything to detract from tourism. Tom had learned how to solve problems quickly and quietly.

"What brings you to see me, Boots?" His deep voice seemed out of place coming from his 5'5" tall body. Immaculately dressed in his Royal Bahamian Police uniform, his small frame belied his true physical strength. The few men who were foolish enough to challenge him quickly found out their mistake, usually lying on their backs.

"Julie's niece, Bebe and her husband Winston are missing. They were due back from their honeymoon cruise a week ago and no one has heard from them."

With a frown on his face, he said "Do you know their itinerary?" Even though I'd only known him a short time, he and Julie had gone to school together, knew Bebe and he had been one of the ushers at her wedding.

No, I don't, Tom. I'm headed over to the Hatchet Bay marina office to find out what I can."

"Let me know what you find out and I'll call the Coast Guard and find out if they have any news." He stood up and came around his desk and reached up to put his hand on my shoulder. I'll do anything I can, Boots. Anything."

"Thanks, I'll let you know right away."

Chapter Four

The Hatchet Bay marina was up the coast a few miles and as I drove north, I enjoyed the view of the calm, blue waters to my left, the water skiers slaloming along and far out, a schooner under full sail running with the wind.

The arrangement of the docks seemed familiar and seeing one of the boat owners taking a fresh caught sailfish off of his boat and laying it on the dock, reminded me of my near miss with a shark. Years ago, a dead shark, lying on its back on a dock had snapped at my ankle as I walked by, terrifying big brave unflappable me. I found out that even when their heart stops, their nervous system keeps working for a while.

I shook my shoulders to get rid of the memory and drove into the marina property and parked by the dock-master's office. The screen door twanged shut as I entered. The room was hot and humid, no air circulation that I could see. A young woman in an off the shoulder, white blouse greeted me with a smile, eyebrows uplifted in question. "Hep ya, suh?" she said, her face wet with perspiration.

"Hi, my name is Boots Beaumont. Friends of mine chartered a boat from you about two weeks ago and they have not returned so I'm worried.

"D'ya mean, Bebe n Wilson?"

"Yes, how did you know?"

"What is your relationship to dem, suh?"

"Julie D'Arville is Bebe's aunt. Julie is a close friend and asked me to inquire since she has not heard from them." Everyone on Eleuthera knew Julie so I knew this would be reason enough to help me.

"Okay, a friend of Julie means you are important man, suh. They called on der VHF radio, asking if they could keep da boat longer."

"They called?" I said in surprise.

"Da mister Winston called, suh."

"Did they say where they were?"

"No, they din't say, suh."

"Did they say how long they wanted to stay out?"

"No, suh, not my business to ask him"

"Did you ask him?"

"No suh, we got the deposit for da charter so we not worried."

"Do you have their filed travel itinerary?"

"Yes suh, it's here in der file. Would you like to see it?"

"Yes, please." This was like pulling teeth and I was getting very annoyed, even though I knew she was not giving me a hard time on purpose. This was undoubtedly how she was trained to respond to customers.

"Here you are suh, " she said as she handed me a printed sheet from a stained manila folder.

The plan said they had chartered the *Lazy Daze*, a 37' Tayana ketch and were going to sail southeast to the Virgins. They had taken on provisions for a two week cruise. They left on January 1st and planned to return on the 31st. It seemed a bit optimistic but reasonable, a week's sail there and a weeks' sail back and two weeks to explore.

"Has the Coast Guard called you about this?"

"No, suh." She turned away, then turned back. "Suh, I don like dis. I jus don like dis."

"Neither do I, Miss, neither do I. Thank you for your help. Have a nice day," I said as I walked out the door, exchanging inside heat for outside heat.

The fact that the Coast Guard hadn't called her didn't bother me. They can be very disorganized but I knew they'd get around to it. The young woman's last words bothered me a lot. I got into my Jeep and drove south towards on what some of us non-Bahamian residents call the Trans-Eleutheran highway.

As I drove, my mind was on the travels of Bebe and Winston. Why didn't they call Julie or Cappy or me? Why? It made no sense. Out of the corner of my eye, I spotted something on the opposite side of the badly rutted road. I screeched to a stop, got out and went across the lane. I saw two tiny striped kittens, curled up and sleeping like bookends under a palmetto tree. When I approached, they must have sensed it as they both looked up a bit, and mewed so softly it was barely audible. I guessed they were starved and dehydrated.

"Hey kitties, are you ok?" At the sound of my voice, their tails stood straight up, the tips bent a bit and their mewing got louder. "Ok, ok. Are you hungry? Would you like to come with me?" Of course, I knew they said "yes" so I scooped them up and put them on the passenger seat. They looked at me, then curled up together, put their heads down and went back to sleep. I started the engine and continued on my way to my marina. I stopped at Martine's grocery store for kitten food, litter and a litter box. I knew I was hooked by these kittens. Hooked with the proverbial line and sinker too. I looked in the rear view mirror and saw that I had a big smile on my face.

From the Eagle Chronicles # 3

"Passing south of Rendezvous Bay. 90 minutes out. Buzzard and Falcon, over."

"Call me when you reach Saint James Island, over," said Eagle

"Roger. Over and out."

Eagle had been drinking a beer on the fantail while watching one of the giant sea turtles swimming close to the surface. The sun was about to set and the horizon was pink over the hills to his west. His salt and pepper hair was more salt these days from the bleaching power of the sun and his hazel eyes were green like the water in Cowpet bay. He idly scratched a mosquito bite on his arm. *"One thing about Buzz, she was always doing what was needed. She never keeps me in the dark. All was well. Ten hours. Time for one more go with Martha. Then nite nite Martha."* Eagle grinned. "Martha? Yo. Get your ass up here."

"Yes, Eagle?" Martha knew what that voice meant and came up on deck with only her bikini bottom on. No words were needed as Eagle rose, took her hand and went below.

A gust of wind from the west buffeted *Raptor* and Eagle was instantly awake. Martha was sleeping on her stomach, sprawled across the king size bed in the master stateroom. *"Might as well do it now while she sleeps,"* thought Eagle and he quickly put his hands under her forehead and just as quickly lifted her head back as far as it would go until he heard the snap of her broken neck. Eagle felt no guilt, only a slight sadness that his little playmate would not be there to please him anymore. He put on his bathing shorts and got one of the old tarps from the storage lockers. He spread it out on the deck, placed a rusty old anchor in the center of it, lifted the now dead Martha from the bed and dropped her on the tarp. He tucked the ends over her head and feet and then rolled it up. He tied the bundle with some spare anchor chain and went up onto fantail. It was dark by now but he wanted to make sure no boats had come close. He went back down, hauled the makeshift burial clothes surrounding Martha topside, quickly lowered her over the side and let go. *"Bye bye, Martha. The sharks will say hello to you soon. I hope they enjoy your company as much as I did."* Eagle went below, took a shower and was instantly asleep.

In the morning, after some coffee, Eagle was watching the southeast tip of Cowpet Bay's inlet, the scent of bougainvillea in the air. The water skiers were already out in the water between St. Thomas and St. John and the wash from one of the ferry boats reached *Raptor* and raised her up and down in sync with the breeze. Buzz and Falcon were due to appear there within the next hour. *"I can't wait to see the new boat. And find some alone time with Buzz too. Martha was great, but Buzz is super. I'll send Falcon off in the zodiac to get some food from the Marina Market in town. Then I'll have him change the name on the new boat. I think I'll name it 'Hornby', yeah. Good idea."*

"Sometimes things work out the way you want them to," Eagle thought as he basked in the Caribbean sun, one eye on the horizon, and one on a cute girl sailing one of the Elysian hotel's rental sunfish. He was thinking about how this adventure got started. After a lot of posts back and forth, Eagle asked how many of the others in the raptor group were angry at society. Buzzard, Hawk, Falcon and Owl responded that they were disenchanted with life in general and angry to boot. Eagle then sent a message to the four other "birds" asking them if they'd like to get together on a vacation and discuss some ideas he had that would enrich all their lives. They all said yes and Eagle suggested that they meet in St. Thomas in the U.S. Virgin Islands. He reserved a suite with 5 bedrooms at the Elysian Hotel on Cowpet Bay.

Eagle took the ferry to the mainland and then a bus to the Vancouver airport where he boarded an Air Canada flight to

Miami, then an American Flight to Charlotte Amalie on St. Thomas. He rented a car and drove across the island to the Elysian so he could get the lay of the land to feel safe. It took him a few minutes to get used to driving on the "wrong" side of the road and then he started to relax. He was wearing tropical clothes so that he would not stand out as a tourist. After he drove through the security gate and as he drove down the hill to the office he could see the island of St. John in the distance. *"Some day I'll own a hunk of beach over there. Some day soon."* He checked in, had a light lunch at Bonnie's open air restaurant. Sitting at his table, he heard a thump on the other side of his table and to his surprise saw a three foot long iguana right itself and scurry away.

"Denis? How did that happen?"

The waiter replied, "Mon, they fall asleep up in the palm trees and fall down. It happens a lot. We've moved all the tables to places where they can't fall on you while they eat. Worry not."

"Thanks, Denis. Do they bite?"

"They'll chase a toe from time to time but they won't really bite it. They don't like the taste," said Denis with a grin.

After his lunch, he went up to the suite and, exhausted from 6 hours of flying took a nap.

In the morning, after a full breakfast of bacon, eggs, juice and coffee, without any falling iguana interruptions, he drove back to the airport to meet the others. He had some time to kill so he stood in the observation area so he could watch the flights come and go. Flying fascinated him. *"I've got to find out their real names and have them sign some kind of agreement, just to be safe. Just in case. I'll sign too but it won't matter. I just may need some leverage in the future. Here comes the US Air flight. That must be the one from Philadelphia. Now to meet the Buzzard."*

"My God, Buzzard is a woman, she's beautiful too," he thought as she walked up to him in baggage claim, put her hand and said, "Hi,

Eagle. I'm Buzzard.   Thanks for putting that flower above your ear so I'd know you."

"Hi, Buzz, nice to meet you."

"How did you know it was ok to call me, Buzz?"

"I don't know, I just knew and I always trust my instincts."

"Good," she said with a smile. "There are my bags, Eagle."

"I'll get them. And we have an hour until the next plane so let's grab some lunch and a drink, ok?"

"Sure, Eagle.. I'm starved. What they served on that flight could hardly be called food."

They walked upstairs to the dining concession overlooking the runways and sat at a table close to the big picture window. Eagle walked behind her and could not keep his eyes off her stunning body. Her soft brown hair and brown eyes only added to his inner excitement.

"Easy, Eagle, easy, she's just another broad. Don't get carried away."

Chapter Five

Yvonne, in one of my blue shirts knotted at the waist over a pair of blue shorts, and Cappy in cutoff jeans were waiting on the afterdeck transom set, sipping wine as I walked up the gangplank with the two kittens cradled in my arms..

"Yo Boots, who're your little friends?" asked Cappy

"Hoe gaat het?" asked Yvonne in Dutch. She rarely spoke Dutch to me so I knew that saying 'Hi' in Dutch meant that she was still in her nomadic mood which worried me... worried me a lot.

"Hey, you two. Say 'Hi' to the kitties. I found them on the side of the road in town. Excuse me while I get a bowl of water for them. Vonnie, would you hold them for me?" Her hands were outstretched before I finished the sentence. Her face was aglow.

I went into the salon, put the litter box on the floor behind one of the chairs, filled it, got two bowls, one full of water one with kitty kibble and brought them back outside and laid them on the deck near Yvonne. The kitties wasted no time lapping up half the bowl of water, alternating with the kibble in the other bowl. I sat on one of the two swivel chairs and leaned back.

Cappy asked, "Well, anything to report my friend?" and they both looked at me expectantly.

"Yes, but wait a sec. Vonnie, would you like to name the kittens?" I knew the answer before she answered. She had the kittens sitting on her lap.

"Ja, I mean, yes. That's easy. This one with the faint orange in her stripes is Pietje and this all gray one is Stafje."

"What do those names mean and how did you do it so fast," asked Cappy

"Well to me this one looks like a little bit of fluff so she is Pietje and the other one looks like a bit of dust, so she is Stafje. That's how those words translate in Dutch." She touched them very lightly on the top of the head each time she said their name.

"Vonnie, you are incredible. They look just like you described," said Cappy.

"I agree. Vonnie, you never cease to amaze me." The kittens must have agreed too as they looked up at Vonnie, put their heads down and fell asleep instantly.

"So, back to my trip." I told them of my visit to the police and the marina. When I finished Cappy said, "That part about them calling in saying they were going to stay longer smells, Boots, it truly stinks."

"I know, Cap, I know." I could see his ex-shrink brain turning my words around in his head and coming to the same conclusion that my ex-PI brain did. Something was wrong, very wrong.

Yvonne said, "We should be worried, yes?"

Cappy and I both said yes at the same time.

Yvonne said, "Well I don't hope so." and got up and stormed off the deck.

"Her English goes to shit when she is upset," mumbled Cappy with a frown on his face. "What can we do?"

"Well, the fact that the Coast Guard has not responded is upsetting so I think it's time to call our old friend at the FBI. Do you agree?"

"I sure do." said Cappy.

I picked up my cell phone and dialed Red Baron's phone number from memory, wondering if I ought to put it on speed dial, considering how often I called him.

"While you are waiting, would you like a glass of white?" asked Cappy.

"Yes, but check on Yvonne first."

"Aye, aye, skipper," came the reply with a grin on Cappy's face.

While waiting for Red to pick up, listening to the FBI music-on-hold, I thought back to how I met him. I helped an adopted person find his original mother and because of that met Red who broke up a baby-selling ring. An emotionally rewarding experience for me, and for Julie as well. We.. "Hello? This is Red Baron, how can I help you?" interrupted my reverie.

"Red, this is Boots. Got a sec?"

"Sure, for you, any time. What's up?"

"Julie's niece, the one whose wedding you were at on New Year's Eve, is missing. She and her husband chartered the *Lazy Daze* a 37' Tayana ketch from the Hatchet Bay marina on January 1st and were due back on the 8th. They are more than a week overdue. Winston's dive shop called them and Lieutenant Thomas Greenslade of the local police called them as well, but they have not yet responded. "

"I know the commander of the local Coast Guard office, Boots and will raise hell. I'll keep you posted."

"Thanks, Red. This means a lot to me. And, say 'Hi' to Suzy for me."

Yvonne and Cappy had come back on deck while I was talking to Red and were sitting on the transom seats. Cappy got up, handed me a glass of my favorite wine, Puilly Fumé de la Doucette, and sat back down next to Yvonne.

I took a sip, took a moment to savor the nutty flavor and said, "Thanks you two. This hits the spot"

"Well? What did he say?" asked Cappy. Yvonne looked on expectantly.

"He had not heard about it but he will put some pressure on the Coast Guard to get this rolling."

"Great, Boots. I'll let Edward know what's going on. I've got some journals to catch up on. So, I'll talk to you later." He leaned over, gave Yvonne a peck on the cheek, came over and gave me a reassuring squeeze on the top of my shoulder and left.

Yvonne asked, "Would you like to see what I bought at the market?"

"Sure, Vonnie, I'd love to."

"Well, you'll have to come below."

"Why not bring it here and show me?"

"It's in our cabin, Boots and I think it would upset some of our neighbors if I brought it up here."

"I'll be right down, Vonnie." I gave the kittens more water and went below smiling, sure to close and lock the hatch behind me.

Chapter Six

"Boots, Are you loving me?"

"I thought I just did that."

She nestled closer to me and punched me lightly in arm. "Not that, silly, I mean loving me?"

"Do you mean do I love you?"

"Yes, isn't that what I just asked, silly man?"

"Well, sort of, Vonnie," I responded with a grin. I was aware of the light rocking of the boat and the sea breeze that came through the master stateroom as I pondered how to answer.

"So?" and another punch on the arm.

"Vonnie, the answer is a qualified yes."

"What is this qualified yes? I don't understand."

"I am afraid to love you, I mean, I love you but I am afraid of loving you because you leave a lot."

"I leave a lot because I am afraid of loving you."

"Why are *you* afraid, lieve Vonnie?"

"I like it when you call me 'dear' in Dutch, lieve Boots. I am afraid that your work is more important than I am so I do things for me to find what I will do in case you leave."

"Why do you think my work is more important than you are?"

"Because you are so intense when you are on a case or writing, that's why." and she gave me a harder punch.

"Ow, that hurt. But only a bit."

"I want all of your attention."

"You have it, Vonnie. And you are more important to me than my work or my writing. And I will not leave you,

"I don't hope so."

"Oh boy. Would you like more of my attention?"

"You mean now?

"Ja."

Chapter Seven

As I opened my eyes, the sun was streaming in the portholes on my right. The boat was gently rocking in the waves of a passing speedboat. My mouth was dry, perhaps from too much of the Puilly Fumé, my eyes a bit sandy. Vonnie's left leg was tangled with my right one. I gently moved, pulled my leg free, got up and went to take a shower. I noticed that the kittens were sleeping between Vonnie's outstretched legs, a ray of sunlight across her nose.

I found I was quietly singing, "I'm saving my money, to buy you a rainbow, a rainbow, to put on your finger. And after I've gone and bought you the rainbow, I'll go out and buy you the moon." *Wow, that's a love song. Holy shit, I think I love her.* How am I going to handle that?

I went into the galley and saw that Vonnie had thoughtfully set the coffee maker on auto so I poured a cup, added some sweetener and went back to the fantail deck. I sat in the sun, lost in thought about Vonnie and how to tell her I love her when she tapped me on the shoulder.

"Good morning, Boots."

"Good morning, Vonnie, how did you sleep?"

"I'm confused. I slept on my side like I always do."

"Oops, that didn't translate. The question means did you have a goed slaap?"

"Ah, yes I did." And she zipped inside the lounge and came back with her note book. "How did you sleep? It means did I have goed slaap?"

"Ja, I mean, yes." She was still standing so I got up and gave her a hug and a kiss.

We were still hugging and I said, "I have some emailing to do, Vonnie. Do you have anything planned for this morning?"

"Yes, some sun and then some kitchen things."

She gave me a kiss that sent smoke out my ears and gently disengaged, sat down and looked up at me with a big smile. I smiled back and went in through the salon to my office to check my email. I had a slew, mostly junk, telling me things like I had won the Australian lottery or that I was heir to a fortune left to me and an uncle I didn't know about in England. I sipped my coffee as I answered a few inquiries for assistance with a polite refusal and before I knew it, it was time for lunch.

I had taught Vonnie how to make my favorite *Pollo Scarpariello* and she surprised me by serving it for lunch. She had learned well, it was delicious.

We finished cleaning up after lunch and went topside, taking some of the Puilly Fumé from the night before with us and were quite relaxed when my cell phone rang.

The kittens woke up to the sound of the phone, rolled over and went back to sleep under Vonnie's captain's chair. Vonnie looked over at me as I took the phone out of its clip on the waist of my cutoffs, cute as a button in her pale blue bikini. Actually it was so small that it was almost a no-kini at all.

I gave Vonnie a wink and said, "Hey Red, I'm surprised to hear from you so soon. What's up?" Yvonne whispered that she was going to take a nap and went below. The kittens stayed behind, under the shade of a deck chair. I took my shirt off and put oil on my back. I could feel the afternoon sun sizzling the oil. The water was quiet but there were a lot of pelicans doing some fishing

"A lot, my friend, a lot."

I could hear the worry in his voice. "Like?" There was the mixed sound of some people talking in the background and paper being shuffled as well.. Pietje was playfully tugging on my sandal straps making little mewing sounds.

"Boots, there have been reports of 5 other couples who have gone missing in the area in the last six months. Two honeymooners sailed from St. John , the 2 college girls sailed from Red Hook on St. Thomas and two other couples, one sailed from St. Croix and one from Tortola. They were all supposed to stay within the general area defined by those islands. They were all reported missing when they did not return as scheduled. The Coast Guard has not been able to find any of them. Julie's niece and her husband make the sixth pair to go missing and the only ones not sailing from the Virgins."

"Good God, Red, what's being done?"

"We, the FBI, and the Coast Guard have sent out bulletins to all travel agencies and airlines and marinas to warn anyone thinking about going cruising in the area until further notice. The Coast Guard has doubled its patrols in the area. Frankly, I'm very worried as we seem to be dealing with some very psyched-up modern day pirates. And they are very hard to catch."

"So, Red, there are no clues? Ouch. Sorry, the kitten just nibbled on my big toe."

"What kitten?"

"I found two abandoned kittens by the side of the road yesterday so I brought them home with me. They are full of the dickens and I need to watch my step as they get underfoot so fast. Mostly that's not a problem as they seem to prefer following Yvonne."

"I truly hate it when people abandon animals. Ok, back to our problem. There is one clue. Last week, one of our men was vacationing on St. Thomas and saw a fuss down at the shore where he was staying. He walked down to the beach and showed his badge to the local fuzz. They reluctantly showed him a piece of a lifejacket that had been discovered. One of the guests at the hotel found it while snorkeling along the shore. It was tangled on a piece of coral. It had the letters *IP* stenciled on it. One of the missing boats was the *Serendipity*, a 34' Trumpy owned by the Paradise Harbor Club marina on Paradise Island chartered by one of the honeymooners."

"Red, St. Thomas is over 800 miles from here."

"Yes, I know, yet there were only a few boats reported missing in the Virgin Islands in the last year and none of them had the letters *IP* as part of their name. And the lifejacket piece looked new."

"You know, Red, I've been wanting to go to St. Thomas for a long time."

"Why do you have to stick your nose in everything? Huh? Huh?" said Red with a trace of anger, "You could get yourself hurt or worse."

"Red worry not, I know how to take care of myself. I just think that Vonnie and the kittens deserve a vacation. Maybe Cappy would want to join us."

"Well, I know I can't change your mind once it's made up. Please be careful, my friend and if you need me call. I'll tell Carl Ricci, the local FBI man in St. Thomas that you'll be in touch."

"Thanks, Red. I'll say 'Hi' as soon as we find a mooring."

"The Elysian Beach Club has a place to tie up for free, Boots. And the American Yacht Club in Redhook is a full service marina. I repeat, Please be careful."

"I will and worry not, we'll be ok." *Sure we would.*

"Hey Vonnie? Want to take a cruise?"

I heard a loud *"Yes"* from somewhere inside my boat. Stafje and Pietje both looked up at me, heads cocked to the side. "Yes, ladies, you can come too, but first we need to take you to Dr. Soda and get you checked out."

From the Eagle Chronicles # 4

Eagle and Buzzard walked to baggage claim side by side to wait for the Delta flight out of Miami. Hawk, Falcon and Owl had all managed to be on the same plane which simplified things.

Lunch had been very pleasant and Eagle had probed as much as he thought he could.

"So what was it like growing up in Scranton, Buzz?"

"Horrid, really, Eagle, horrid."

"Why? What was bad about it?"

She shuddered and said, "Getting hit all over by my dad for the slightest thing and then having the nuns who hit too, with rulers sometimes. I got hit so badly I still have scars on my arms."

"Sorry, Buzz. I know about getting hit."

They were both silent as they waited for their sandwiches to arrive.

"Say, Buzz? I'll show you mine if you show me yours."

"What? Are you kidding with that old line?"

Eagle laughed. "I mean, I'll tell you my real name if you tell me yours"

"Oh, sure, "she said smiling. "Cathy Parsley. Can you believe it? I hated it because I got teased so much. And yours?"

"Stephen Gage," said Eagle. *"Damned if anyone will know who I am."*

"How did you pick the name, Buzzard?"

"I always got the leftovers, Eagle, always. Three brothers and two sisters and I was the youngest. Sometimes I even had to wear my brothers' old clothes. And you… How did you pick Eagle?"

"I would have *had* the hand-me-downs but I just swooped in and took what I wanted. I got hit for it but I always got mine."

"Delta 501 from Miami, now arriving at gate one. Passengers will arrive through Area B," came the voice over the speaker system.

"We are in the right place so in a few minutes, we'll meet our new friends."

"Good," said Buzzard. "I'm psyched."

"So am I," said Eagle as he admired Buzz's outfit, walking shorts, loose batik blouse and a pastel band around her blonde ponytail. Her blue eyes were hidden behind her sun glasses.

Buzz pointed to the custom's door. "Those three must be ours. What do you think?" She was almost whispering and Eagle responded in kind.

"I told them to look for the rose in my hair so they'll spot us for sure."

The three men walked directly to Eagle and Buzz.

"Hi, I'm Hawk," said the tallest and most slender of the three newcomers, putting out his hand.

Eagle and Buzz shook his hand and said "Hi' in return.

An almost rotund man, about five and a half foot tall, said, "Hey, I'm Owl." and almost at the same time, "Hi, I'm Falcon," was heard from an average looking man with a hooked nose. Both of them put their hands out and Eagle and Buzz took turns shaking hello.

"Nice to meet you guys, I'm Eagle and this is Buzzard."

"Your baggage will arrive at Carousel two," said Eagle with one eye on Buzzard to see if she was paying any particular attention to them. *"Good. She is not showing any signs of interest."*

Chapter Eight

I went below to the salon where Vonnie was slipping on her sandals.

"I'm glad you changed out of that bikini, Vonnie."

"You didn't like it?" she said with a puzzled look on her face.

"Oh, I liked it but you could have gotten arrested for inciting a riot of the male population of Eleuthera." I told her with a huge grin. I like your shorts and blouse just fine."

"I will remember that if I feel like causing trouble in the future.

Boots?"

"Yes?"

"You honor me by letting me choose Dutch names for the kittens. Danke, thank you."

 "My pleasure. Vonnie.

Vonnie picked up the kittens and followed me through the aft doorway and down the gangplank to the dock. We walked hand in hand to the parking lot. They were so small that her other hand could hold both of them.

We got in the jeep, drove out of the marina and turned right onto Queen's Highway for the 5 minute ride to the vet's office on Bay Street.   The sun was splashing through palm leaves to make quickly vanishing designs on the windshield as we moved.

"What kind of name is 'Soda', asked Vonnie?"

"Dr. Soda is Japanese. He was written up in the local paper. His grandfather, at the end of World War Two, wanted to get as far from Japan as he could to be free. He looked up the word "freedom" and Eleuthera came up as one of the matches. Eleuthera is a girl's name in Greek that means "freedom" so he took his wife and young son, moved here and opened up a veterinary office. He struggled financially for quite a while but he managed to save enough money to send his son to the University of Miami veterinary school. His son came back and joined him in his practice.

In 1980, his son got married to a Bahamian woman, Angelique and in 1981, gave birth to Hideki Soda. Three months after Hideki was born, his mother, father and grandfather were killed when a small plane crashed into their boat while they were coming home from a day of shopping in Nassau. Hideki had been with Berenice, Angelique's mother who loved to babysit for her only grandchild. There was no question that she would raise him and Hideki's father had an insurance policy to ensure he would be well taken care of. Angelique's mother was included in the policy, just in case. Hideki excelled in school and got a scholarship to U of Miami like his dad. Berenice made sure that Hideki visited the graveside whenever he wished, told him stories about his mother, father and grandfather and made sure he grieved their deaths."

Yvonne had tears in her eyes and said, "How sad for him, Boots. What kind of man is he?"

"He is a very delightful man, Vonnie full of fun, loved by many on this island. He does a very unique thing."

"What's that, Boots?"

"Whenever he emails or leaves a message he signs or says his name like this… 'delightedSoda' or 'regretfulSoda' or 'sincereSoda'."

"That is so cute."

"Yes, and here we are," I said as we pulled into Soda's parking lot on Bay Street. He bought the one story building long ago and has modernized it to suit his growing practice. There is a BMW convertible with SODA on the license plate. I guess he is doing well.   We got out and walked to the door.

The well-lit air-conditioned waiting room was empty and the receptionist, a pleasant looking Bahamian woman, greeted us. "Good afternoon folks, hey kitties. What can I do for you today?"

"Our new kittens, Stafje and Pietje, would like to see Dr. Soda" The kittens were looking at me, then Vonnie, then the receptionist, then the room, back and forth with apprehension.

She said, "He is just finishing up a phone call, so come on into the exam room," and opened a door to a 10 x 12 room with a steel table in the center. "He'll be right in," and walked out.

She meant it. The door had not been shut for a second when Dr. Soda walked in and said, "HappySoda is pleased to meet you," and held out his hand and Vonnie and I shook it, saying our names. He was about 5'9, slender with an engaging smile. I liked him immediately.

"Hey kitties, what're your names," and scooped each one up from where I had set them on the table as I introduced them, then put them back down.

"What brings Stafje and Pietje to us today?"

"I found them yesterday on the side of the road near the Hatchet Bay Marina. I want to make sure they are healthy."

"Well, let's take a look." He proceeded to examine them, front and back. "They sure look healthy enough. I want to run a blood-panel to be sure and we'll give them their shots too." He took out a syringe to take the blood and Yvonne walked out of the room. They did not make a sound as Dr. Soda drew blood and gave them their shots.

"Mr. Beaumont, I..."

"Call me Boots."

"Boots, they look to be in very good condition, even though a bit dehydrated. I'll have the results of the blood tests back tomorrow afternoon. I don't think you have to worry. And by the way, they are lucky you found them. Very lucky." He smiled and held out his hand.

I shook it and said, "Thanks, Dr. Soda, a pleasure meeting you."

"Please call me Soda." He opened the door and held it as I scooped the kitties off the table and held them in my hand. I handed them to Yvonne who had been waiting in the reception area.

I paid the receptionist, went out to the jeep, went to the local grocery store across from the police station to buy some fresh fish for dinner and drove back to the *Lost & Found.*

Chapter Nine

I called Cappy and left a message telling him to come over for dinner. Yvonne marinated the fish and made a salad. The kittens had decided they needed to sleep on the settee in my office where I sat lost in thought.

I knew that many people disappear in the Caribbean area each year but eight in just six months in the Virgins seemed like a lot. I hoped it was just coincidence but my guts said, "no". I heard Cappy arrive and went into the salon to greet him. He was sitting on the deck, playing with the kittens. Somewhere Cappy had produced a toy mouse and was trying to teach the kittens how to fetch.

"Yo, Cap. How goes it?"

"I'm well and I'm pleased to be here for what my nose tells me will be a sumptuous dinner but the kittens are slow to learn how to fetch."

And with that, Yvonne said, "Dinner is served, gentlemen."

Cappy and I sat at the table, which was set with a pastel striped table cloth, striped plates, striped napkins. I expected to be served Striped Bass. Yvonne put a teak salad bowl filled with spinach salad and a warm bacon dressing and no sooner had we devoured that when she produced sautéed swordfish covered with a lemon butter sauce with capers. With a smile on her face, she poured a nice white zinfandel into each of our glasses. This felt like being in first class on a plane.

We did not speak during the meal; It was too good to interrupt with speech. When all of us had placed our silverware on the plates, I broke the silence.

"Cappy, do you want to know what I found out from Red today?"

"I thought you'd never ask, Boots. What gives?"

Yvonne started to clear the table.

"Wait, Vonnie, we'll all do that. I want you to be part of this discussion."

Cappy sat back, his intent eyes focused on my face as I told him what I had learned.

"What do you think, Cap?"

"I'd like to know what you think first, Boots."

"My God, you are always the shrink, aren't you? Zeeeeeeeeech."

"I'm not playing shrink. I just have a hunch that it's important for you to speak first."

"Gee thanks, doc," I said with a grin. "What I think is that the three of us need to take a cruise to St. Thomas ASAP."

"Why? And why do you want me to be included?"

"The Virgin Islands are clearly the common denominator of all these disappearances. St. Thomas is where the lifejacket was found so it seems like a good starting point. And you can surely be our profiler, Cap. Besides, I can use the extra hand."

"Well, I'll go but only because I think you two need a chaperone"

"What is a chaperone?" asked Yvonne.

"A chaperone is someone who accompanies young people on a date to make sure they don't do things their parents don't want them to do," said Cappy.

"It means that Cappy could stop us from doing things," I said.

"I don't hope so," said, Yvonne who walked out of the salon giggling.

"Ok, Cappy. You are on. I'd like to leave the day after tomorrow at first light if that works for you. I need a day to get provisions and fuel and arrange for my mail to be held"

"Aye aye, Cap'n."

Chapter Ten

The next morning, when I came back from taking a walk, Yvonne had made toast and coffee for us and put some fresh food in the kitties' dish. They had adjusted well to their new home and seemed to always be at Yvonne's heels, mewing with their tails a'wavin. Yvonne clearly liked this adoration.

Yvonne and I spent the rest of the day getting enough food for ten days. I had figured out that running at 9 knots was about a little over 10 miles per hour which meant that if we cruised 18 hours a day, we could make St. Thomas in about four and a half days using only half our fuel capacity. That was a comfortable estimate allowing for unforeseen problems which always seemed to develop on a boat at sea. So, we topped off the four fuel tanks and filled our two fresh water tanks as well.

"Yvonne, will you put the groceries away while I check the batteries and the generator? I want to check all the running lights and electronics as well."

"You bet, Skipper, anything else you want me to do for you?"

"Oh, I might think of something before Cappy comes back at dinnertime," and quickly backed out of the salon giving her a lascivious grin before ascending the spiral stairs to the pilot house. I was afraid I'd forget so I called Red's cell phone and got his answering service.

"Red, Boots here. Cappy and I are leaving in the morning for St. Thomas. We plan to arrive in about five days so let your local guy Ricci know that I'll be in touch. You can reach me on the VHF if anything new develops before we check in. Thanks, Red."

I turned on all the running lights and went out the starboard door for a walk-around. The running lights were all aglow. While I was at it, I checked the pressure gauge on the zodiac runabout to be sure it was fully inflated and checked the gas tank on its outboard engine.

I went back down the spiral staircase to the salon and then went down the stairs to the engine room. I checked the oil in each engine and the auxiliary generator and the fluid level in each battery as well.

I went back up to the salon where I could, looking over the dividing pass-through counter, see Yvonne as she was just finishing up organizing our provisions. She was a very good at it whereas I was just plain awful at it. The kittens were lying on the aft end of the settee in the salon directly opposite the galley, their heads on their paws, eyes focused on Yvonne.

She took one look at my grease smeared face and said, "You are dirty man, very dirty. I will not talk to you until you take a shower."

"Would you help me scrub?" and headed for the shower, smugly knowing that she was right behind me."

Chapter Eleven

Cappy came for dinner bearing his over-the-shoulder bag and Chinese carry-out.

"Cappy, how can you manage a month's worth of clothing in that small bag? I'd need a large valise."

"It's a trade secret my friend, but I'll give you a hint. Think Zen."

"Forget Zen, I'm thinking the Sesame Chicken. I'll leave Zen alone. And, I'd need two big suitcases," said Yvonne.

We made small talk during our meal. Yvonne and I used forks while Cappy used chopsticks.

"Cappy? Why are you using chopsticks when using a fork like Boots and me is so much easier?"

"Yvonne, my dear, think.."

And before he could finish, Yvonne and I both said, "Zen."

We all laughed and then got down to business. Cappy agreed to be in charge of the rigging. It was automatic but he was to make sure that when we raised our sails that the lines did not get snarled. Yvonne, who loved cooking, agreed to be in charge of feeding us as well as keeping our ship's log up to date. My job was navigation and general seagoing tasks, especially making sure that all of the boat's systems were functioning well. I also told them that I'd keep our VHS on so we could be contacted at any time, especially by Red.

As much as I loathed doing so, I showed them where I kept my rifle and pistol hidden. The rifle was under the port settee in my lounge and the pistol was in a clip under the dashboard just starboard of the wheel.   I was not a fan of firearms but being an ex-PI I knew that shit happened and I wanted to be ready.

"I see the looks on your faces, let's go out on the fantail," I suggested as I walked aft. They both followed.

"Why are you showing us these ugly things, Boots?" asked Yvonne.

"I fucking hate guns, Boots. You know that." said Cappy.

"Yes, you two, I know, but…"

"But?" they said, almost in unison.

"The *but* is that eight people have gone missing and we are cruising in an area where two of them sailed. I want us to be ready to protect ourselves, just in case."

"I don't like this *just in case."* said Yvonne.

"I don't either but in the morning, I'm going to show you two how to use the weapons. How about a nightcap?" I said.

"My head is not cold." quipped Yvonne.

We shared some Sambucca while sitting on the fantail in a gentle breeze, lost in thought.

"I think it's time we turned in. We've got to be up in not so many hours," I said.

"Goodnight you two," said Cappy who turned and gave Yvonne a hug.

I said, "Night Cap."

"Vonnie, we need to go to sleep too."

"Only sleep?"

Chapter Twelve

We were up at the crack of dawn, all wearing cutoffs and light T-shirts, each of us doing our agreed upon jobs. I started the engines and put them on idle and then signaled Yvonne to throw off the bow lines. I signaled Cappy to throw off the stern lines and I put us into forward gear going almost north and bore hard left until we were on a course of 195°, aiming just west of Powel Point at the tip of Eleuthera.

Cappy stowed the lines and then joined me on the bridge. Yvonne brought us coffee and we settled into our routine.

I flipped the switch that automatically hoisted the sails, main first, then stay, then mizzen. Cappy did a walk-around to check that the sails were deployed properly and came back to bridge. Yvonne kept an eye out for other boats. The number of collisions in open water is startling... it happens because no one is looking out for other traffic.

"So you know, we will hold our present course until we've passed Powel Point and then swing east to 175° until we reach Dead Man's Cay on Long Island, about 190 miles.

"Now, how about I show you two how to use your weapons if, God forbid, you need to?" I reached under the dashboard and took out the pistol.

"Yvonne, here is your pistol. Keep it pointed at the deck. Cappy would you go and get the rifle from the salon?" I waited until he had the rifle in his hand, pointing down.

"Cappy, to use the pump action rifle, you hold it up so you can look just over the barrel. Line up the two sights and point that line where you want to shoot. This button is the safety lock.

Yvonne, just point the pistol where you want it to shoot as if you were pointing at someone with your index finger. This button is the safety lock.

Now, I'd like both of you to go out on the fantail, stand on the starboard side, facing west and fire a few rounds each to get the feel of the gun and how much effort it takes to pull the trigger. Better you find out now then if you are in a bad situation and are not sure. Before you fire, make sure you cannot see any boats to starboard."

If they only knew what I had done with a pistol, long ago, another lifetime back in college. In my junior year, during a frat party, two policemen showed up. Springer and Studenbarger. They came to say hello. They wanted a beer. They wanted to talk privately. They wanted a place to hang out when they got bored during their beat. Who were we to say no to them? They became regulars at our parties and just hung around during the day as well. They kept an extra set of clothes in the frat house so they could take off their uniforms and relax. They became friends of a sort. I did the most insane, stupid, dangerous, moronic thing I have ever done in my life, before or since. I was studying in ,my room, Springer asked if could take a shower. He had left his holstered 38 in my room with his uniform. I took the gun out, removed the bullets, cocked the hammer and put a pencil, eraser first into the barrel. When he came back into the room, I pointed the gun at him, said, "Bang. Bang." and pulled the trigger. The pencil flew out and Springer turned white as a sheet. Breathing fast, he sat down, almost collapsed, and asked me in a very controlled voice how I could think that was an ok thing to do. I apologized profusely, not realizing then how truly stupid it was. I think anyone else would have beaten me up and charged me with God knows what crime. "Bang Bang, indeed." I shook my head in self-disbelief.

Cappy went out, took a few shots, then went forward to put the rifle back under the settee and returned.

Yvonne also went and took a few shots, then came back up to the bridge and handed me the pistol which I took down and put in its clip under the dash in the pilot house."

"I could never shoot someone, Boots. No fucking way." said, Cappy.

"Yeah, me the same," said Yvonne who did not swear.

I hope you never have to but, if you do have to take out the guns, you need to be able to pull the trigger.

"Boots, listen.," said, Yvonne.

"Motorsailor, Lost & Found, Coast Guard requests response. Come in, motorsailor, Lost & Found, come in please."

"Shit." I thumbed the switch to turn on the mike at full duplex. "This is Boots Beaumont aboard the motorsailor Lost & Found."

"Boots, this is Red. The Coast Guard was kind enough to patch me in. Can you talk?"

"Sure, what's up?"

"We've got another couple missing, Boots., the thing is…" and he hesitated.

"Yes?"

"They started as a threesome."

"Started? A threesome?"

"Yes, Boots, one guy and two girls."

"Red, what are you not saying?"

"Well, they found the body of a young woman… she got snagged in a fishing net before sunrise this morning, probably not dead for more than a few minutes, literally. We think she jumped overboard and right into the net of the passing trawler as it was being hauled in. And, Boots, she was missing an arm."

"Missing?"

"Yes, it looked like it had been sawed off."

"Sawed off? S A W E D?"

Chapter Thirteen

Yvonne and Cappy sat on the transom mesmerized, eyes wide, hands intertwined, still as stone.

"Boots, somehow she must have been caught unaware, been topside and the lunatic took a swipe at her with a chainsaw. Completely severed her arm and she jumped or fell overboard and bled out immediately. The sharks would have gotten her if she hadn't gotten snagged in the fishing net."

"How do you know she was from the boat with the other two?"

"She had an ID bracelet on her remaining arm. Inside it was her social security number. When the Coast Guard got the info from the trawler, they found her name and contacted her parents. Her parents said she went out with the other two a week ago and had not been heard from since.. They sailed from St. Croix on of all things, a houseboat. We are trying to contact the parents of the missing couple. And guess what?"

"I'm in no mood for guessing, Red. Out with it."

"The body was found near Great St. James Island which is not far from where the life jacket washed up on shore."

"Thanks, Red. Thanks a whole hell of a lot."

"That's what friends are for. Stay safe, Boots. Sounds like madmen out there."

"Cappy, Yvonne, are you ok?"

"I feel sick to my stomach, Boots. How could anyone do such a thing? How?" and she broke into tears. I went to Yvonne and held her, sobbing, until the spasms stopped.

"Boots, sounds like you are dealing with a sociopath, maybe more than one I'd guess. And, yeah, I'm ok. I'm used to hearing these kind of things but it is never easy. May I make a suggestion?".

"Sure, fire away."

"Make a chart, Boots. Talk to Red and get as much info as you can on the missing people and see what they might have in common. It might help us find them."

"Us?"

"Yes, Us. You are not in this alone, my friend, not by a long shot. Didn't you know? Friends that travel to St. Thomas together, solve mysteries together."

Yvonne looked up and smiled while wiping a tear.

"No, I didn't know. I'll have to write that down." I smiled and said, "Who wants lunch? Cappy, please check the rigging, and Yvonne would you update the ship's log and create a gourmet delight?"

"Aye aye, Captain, sir." said Yvonne and went forward into the salon.

"Aye aye, Captain, sir." said Cappy and went aft to check the staysail.

I'd been keeping an eye on our progress and I recognized Powel Point on the port side. As soon as I swung us east to a heading of 175, I reset the autopilot. We were making good time and about at the half way mark for our day's journey.

I still had 3 bars on my cell, so I called Red directly instead of going thru the Coast Guard. I got his voice mail.

"Red, Boots here. Cappy came up with a suggestion. Can you get me the demographics on each of the missing couples? Maybe we'll find a pattern. Also, I'm not happy talking thru the Coast Guard unless there is a secure channel. Whoever is doing this could well be monitoring the CG frequencies. If there is no secure channel, try my cell or send me an email. Thanks, buddy."

I hung up feeling very uneasy about this. *How could I find out what was going on without endangering Yvonne and Cappy? How?*

From the Eagle Chronicles # 5

While they walked to baggage claim, Eagle had noticed that Falcon, Owl and Hawk stayed close together, talking as they walked, while Buzzard stayed close behind him as he led his small group. *"They formed a friendship on their flight, best I keep an eye on that for the future."*

After a few beeps, the carousel started to move and the new arrivals watched for their bags, quickly retrieving them and all eyes turned to Eagle as he said, "This way, lady and gentlemen. Welcome to St. Thomas."

They walked out of the coolness of the terminal into the mildly humid air and across to the parking lot to the rental Chevy wagon. Hawk and Falcon had one bag each, while Owl had two. In contrast, Buzz had arrived with only an under-seat bag on wheels. He clicked the remote and they went to the rear hatch and put in their luggage. Everyone except Buzzard. She took her bag with her and hopped in the passenger seat.

"So where are we off to, Eagle?" asked Falcon as Eagle started to drive out of the airport..

"The Elysian Beach Resort Hotel, about 40 minutes east of here."

"Why there?" asked Owl.

"I found it on line. It's quiet, with good food and a nice air about it."

"Hey. Jesus. You're driving on the wrong side of the road." said Falcon.

"Easy guy, all the roads are this way in the Virgin Islands. It may be U.S Territory but they have their own ideas about roads."

"What the hell is that thing?" asked Hawk, as a blur dashed across the road in front of them, narrowly missing being hit.

"An iguana. They are everywhere and one has to be careful not to hit them. They are not very bright about cars." said Eagle.

"Buzzard is sure quiet but watching and listening to everything, that's for sure." thought Eagle as he was entering downtown Charlotte Amalie.

"This is beautiful downtown Charlotte Amalie shopping on the left and cruise ships on the right." Several large cruise ships were docked and festively adorned with flags and banners. *"Must be several thousand at one time on one of those, I wonder if one day we could. . . ."*

He made the hard right as route 30 went up a hill just past Havensight shopping mall and continued on the winding road, up and down hills. They had all the windows open and the fragrant air was refreshing, even in the heat. They were all quiet, taking in the beauty of the island. "Almost there," said Eagle as they turned right onto Route 322. Soon they turned through stone pillars and an open iron fence and Eagle waved at the guard as they went in drove down a steep drive, then turned right and parked.

"Grab your things and follow me," said Eagle as he walked up a few steps and turned into an open-air corridor. He held out his hand. "Here are your keys. 501 is my room and our meeting room. Buzzard, you are in 502, Falcon 503, Owl 504, Hawk 505. Take some time to freshen up and let's meet in 501 in an hour."

Eagle went into 501 through the living room with its brightly colored cushions on bamboo furniture to his bedroom and took a quick shower. He dressed in white shorts, a sleeveless madras shirt and sandals. He took an iced tea from the fridge, walked through the living room and sat out on the terrace overlooking Cowpet Bay. Dozens of sailboats and motor-yachts bobbing at anchor with the island of St. John in the distance. "It's like having the key to a candy-store, " he said out loud. *"I have to stop thinking that way."*

"I wonder what she is doing in there," thought Eagle, knowing that the door just before the kitchen area connected to Buzzard's room. There was a knock at the door to the suite.

"Doors open. Come in and leave the door open, " said Eagle as he walked back into the living room and sat down in a chair facing in front of the open door.

Owl walked in and said, "Hi-ya"

"Hey Owl, grab a seat."

"Hey, cool digs, Eagle."

Falcon and Hawk walked in together almost immediately followed by Buzzard..

"Take seats folks, get comfy," said Eagle as he sat facing them.

Falcon and Hawk sat on the couch, Owl at the dining room table and Buzz sat on one of the other bamboo chairs. They were all looking at Eagle with anticipation.

"So, I know you are all wondering why we are here. First I have a question for all of you. Did any of you ever think of what it would be like to be a pirate?"

Chapter Fourteen

Cappy was standing with me on the bridge. We were both enjoying the breeze and also watching the horizon for other traffic since Yvonne was below in the galley.

Pietje and Stafje were hanging out in the lounge, mostly curled up on one corner of the sofa. This seemed to be the way they could see Yvonne often and stay cool in the air-conditioned cabin.

Out of the corner of my eye, I saw someone parasailing, the motor of their tow boat a slight buzz in the distance. For a brief moment, I wondered if it was a local or a tourist. A few lost gulls screeched, a discarded Sprite bottle sparked as it bobbed in the slight chop caused by a convenient northwesterly breeze, but angering me that someone had been so disrespectful of the sea.

"Boots, Cap, lunch is ready," came the voice from fantail, behind and below us. Yvonne had set the table with a pastel orange table cloth, clamped to make sure our lunch would not blow away on a magic carpet.

Cappy and I went down and had a seat. Yvonne had prepared a tuna salad with Belgian endive and a pitcher of iced tea with lime. We were quiet, enjoying the very delicious lunch and deep in our own thoughts.

So, I broke the ice. "I've been thinking, you two. I need to run something past you."

They both nodded, eyes wide, and alert.

"It seems to me that we are most at risk at night and then only if we anchor to rest. I suppose we could be at risk while moving but I doubt it. So, I suggest that we do not stop as planned, rather take shifts and sail 24/7. What say ye?"

Yvonne shuddered and said, "Boots, you are the captain and I trust your judgment."

Cappy was quiet, leaning back, chin almost on his chest, legs outstretched under the table."

Cap, your thoughts?"

His head snapped up, opening his eyes as if he was just waking up. "Sorry, I was on top of the mountain."

"Mountain?" said Yvonne. I'd heard him tell of this before so I remained silent.

"Yvonne, I imagine that I am on top of a mountain, on a vast plateau. It is silent. Across the plateau I see someone who I know is a wise, caring person. We walk towards each other and meet in the center. I look into this person's eyes and feel love, understanding and healing energy. I ask the person for guidance and take what I hear to heart. I do it often. Anyone can do it with a bit of practice. Doing this can give us amazing guidance when we are 'stuck'"_

"Wow, Cappy, I'm going to try it when I get a chance," said Yvonne with a big grin.

"I'm glad, Yvonne. Boots, I think you've made a wise decision. I'd love to take midnight to 8am if that works for you."

"Actually, four hour shifts usually work better since after 4 hours one's attention is likely to not be as sharp."

"Okay, would 4 to 8 am work?"

"Sure, Cappy and I'll do midnight to 4. Yvonne , are you ok with 8pm to midnight?"

"Oui mon capitain." she added with a grin.

"Well, you two might want a snooze and now is a good time."

"I'll stay up here for a while, Boots," said Cappy.

"I think I will take a nap and then start dinner. Ciao guys," said Yvonne and she disappeared into the salon so she could go below into the master stateroom, directly below us.

"Boots, I waited for Yvonne to go below before I said what I really think."

I nodded for him to continue.

"I think we are in grave danger from the worst kind of criminal. For sure they are sociopaths. There must be two at least, perhaps three. But two makes more sense. And there has to be someone running this, coordinating the attacks. What if they have informants at the marinas in question, on the alert for young people who are going to sail in specific areas? What if they were told why we are on the move?"

As I pondered what his 'what ifs', I heard the sound of the wind snapping the halyards against the mast and it reminded me of that dead shark snapping at my leg. I thought I was past the terror of that. I guess I need to talk to Cappy about it.

"Boots? Are you there? You seem to have gone space-travelling."

"Wow, yes. I was lost in my head, Cappy, thinking of that dead shark snapping at my ankle long ago. I think I was trying to avoid what you asked me."

"Well?"

"I agree with you as to the number of people directly involved, Cap. With another if. What if there is more than one 'team' doing the pirating? Seems to me that there is a 'team' here and another one in the Virgins as well. And if there are people tipping them off, those people must be rewarded financially so, what is the gain here? The only thing I can think of is that the stolen boats are being sold."

"I agree, Boots, so the questions that arise are, who is doing the selling? From where? And, to whom? You didn't mention my suggestion that *they* know about us, my friend. How come?"

"Because I'm not sure what we can do about it, if they are on the alert for us, other than being extra cautious, especially at night. However, I do not think anyone can sneak up no us while we are running at full speed, Cap."

"I hope you are right. So, show me how you do that Sudoku thing again? I'd like to learn."

"I need to adjust our course, Cap, so look read a little bit of this Sudoku for Dummies."

"Are you giving me a message?"

"Me, giving you a message? Let me get back to you on that."

"Meanwhile, would you put the Sudoku aside for a moment and keep an eye on the rigging? I'm about to make a course change."

I had seen that we are just about to pass the southern tip of Long Island so I set the autopilot to 154°, aiming us just west of Crooked Island. From there we'd change to 117° for a straight shot past the Turks and Caicos Islands to the northern edge of the Dominican Republic. We were making good time and I wanted us to be as far from the Bahamas as possible. It was one of my hunches and I always listened to my gut. Well, almost always.

"All's well, Boots. I'm back to the Sudoku book."

"Enjoy. I'm going below to take a shower before dinner. I can smell the Putanesca sauce from up here."

From the Eagle Chronicles # 6

"Pirate? Like Bluebeard?" asked Owl with a big grin.

"Yes, Like Bluebeard," replied Eagle. "Modern day of course. We wouldn't want to skip the amenities."

The others were silent. "Let's go get some dinner while you mull it over," said, Eagle who promptly stood up and walked to the door. He didn't need to say follow me. They *knew* he was the leader. He had made a reservation for the five of them at Bonnie's. They walked down the hill, a light breeze carrying the mixed smells of the ocean and tropical plants. A dozen or so diners were scattered in the open air restaurant, island music playing lightly in the background. They were given a round table close to the water. Eagle quickly sat facing the water. Buzz sat on his right, Falcon on his left, Owl next to Falcon and Hawk between Buzz and Owl. They ordered drinks and were silent. "Ladies and gents, let's just enjoy our meals. You can think over my question and we'll discuss it upstairs after dinner."

They chit-chatted until dinner was served and then fell silent, each of them intent on their food. Every so often Eagle thought he felt Buzz's left leg touch his but it was like a feather brushing him so he could not be sure though he sure did like the brief sensation. She looked at him no more often than she looked at the others, yet he was sure she was attracted to him a lot. It was clear to him that Owl and Hawk were about to pair off and that pleased him. It left him only Falcon to worry about and worry about him he did. He just had bad vibes and he trusted his vibes.

He had arranged for the bill to be put on his room tab so when they finished their coffees, he said, "Shall we?" and stood and led the way back up the hill to their suite Owl and Buzz behind him with Falcon and Hawk walking side by side in the rear. He unlocked the door, turned on the lights and said, "Have a seat, get comfortable. It's time to get down to business."

"If any of you wish to leave, now is the time. No hard feelings, you've had a nice little time on me. If you stay, you are in for good, understood?" He watched the faces for any signs of a problem. He focused on each of them in turn and each of them nodded and smiled as he met their eyes.

"Ok, so here's the deal. I propose that we carefully pick vacationing couples and steal their boats and sell them on the black-market."

"Sell the boats or the people?" asked Owl, seemingly relaxed in a cushioned swivel chair, his powder green shirt buttoned almost to his throat, indigo colored jeans touching his pristine white sneakers.

"Good questions, Owl. We will sell the boats, not the people."

"What do we do with the people, Eagle?" asked Falcon.

"We make sure that they cannot interfere with our plans," said Eagle, "Is that clear?"

He waited, watching their eyes. "So, to begin with we needed a base of operation and for that, I needed to find a nice floating home. Tomorrow we will check out of here and move into that home. Any questions?"

"Yes," asked Owl who seemed to be the "thinker" of the group, "How will we find the boats to make ours?"

"I will explain all that tomorrow when we are in our new nest. Go get some sleep, you will need it."

Owl nodded, the others arose and walked out, Falcon and Hawk together, then Owl. Buzzard was at the door when she turned around and looked at Eagle.

"Buzz?"

"Got a sec, Eagle?"

"For you?"

"Who else?"

"Who else indeed?" said Eagle with a big grin. "Who else?"

"I just wanted to ask, if I wanted to go home now, could I do that?" asked Buzzard.

"You could ask, Buzz," said Eagle.

"And then?" asked Buzzard.

"I suggest it would be a bad thing to ask," said Eagle.

"Oh," said, Buzzard, "Well, good night, Eagle." Buzzard walked out the door.

"Fuck," said Eagle in a quiet rage.

Chapter Fifteen

There was a steady chop and the wind had shifted to the northeast and I could feel the storm brewing in the air. Yvonne had prepared a meal of salad, spaghetti with Putanesca sauce and meat balls and garlic bread. We made small talk, which was becoming difficult due to the rising sound of the wind with an occasional clap of thunder.

We were drinking coffee when I said, "Up on the bridge and in the wheelhouse, I have portable air horns, small cans of compressed gas, each with a horn on it. If for any reason you think you are in danger, push the button. The sound will alert us that there is a problem and we will come to you ASAP, ok?"

"Thanks, Boots. I like knowing that," said Cappy.

"Me too, Boots, "said, Yvonne.

"Yvonne, thanks for the delicious meal. Cappy and I will clean up. It's your watch in a few minutes. Then mine, then Cap. I'll be in the wheelhouse with you, working on my laptop. I'm thankful for satellite technology."

"I thank you too, Yvonne," said Cappy as he went into the galley

"Okey dokey, I've got the helm as the books say." Yvonne went aft in the cabin to the stairs up to the wheelhouse.

I went to help Cappy clean up, whistling the 'Rainbow' song.

"What's that you're whistling, Boots, I don't recognize it?"

"It's 'Rainbow' an oldie written by George Harrison."

"Why did that pop into your head?" a

"Oh, I don't know, it just did."

We finished the dishes quietly when Cappy said, "This sounds like it could be a hell of a blow, Boots."

"I agree so let's reef the sails and proceed on motor only."

"I'm on it, Boots. We went aft and up to the wheelhouse."

"What's up you two?

"I'm reefing the sails. They need to lowered n during a storm, and Cappy is going on deck to make sure they roll up well." I flipped the switches to activate the motors to take in and the sails, keeping an eye on Cappy for any signal something might be wrong.

"All's well, Skipper," said, Cappy as he came into the wheelhouse.

"Good. Go get some rest, you've got your shift at 4 and 4 rolls around early."

"Aye aye." He went below.

"Yvonne, the autopilot ought to keep us on course but check it and keep an eye out for other traffic at all times. If you see any boats without lights, sound the horn immediately. I'm checking the navigation charts for the Virgins."

I went to my laptop and found the nav charts for the Virgins, remembering that we had to buy them, unroll them and weight them down to keep them flat. Part of my mind was occupied with our route to St. Thomas, the other part of my mind wondering where one would hide stolen boats. Yet another part of my mind was wondering where and how one would sell them and deliver them.

The storm was howling with bursts of lightning off to our west and I looked over at Yvonne. She was sitting in the captain's swivel chair, very intent on the instruments and moving he head from side to side to see what was going on outside in the fast-fading light. The sunset was beautiful and we were riding well. The kittens were so terrified of the storm that they were hiding behind the curtain in the bathtub.

"Boots?"

I'm saving my money, to buy you a rainbow, a rain bow, to put on your finger. And after I've gone and bought you the rainbow, I'll go out and buy you the moon. I woke up thinking I had been singing it out loud. Why am I fixated on that song? I was lying on the settee in the wheelhouse, my laptop was closed, lying on the chart table. I blinked my eyes, "hmmm, whassup?"

"Boots, time to get up for your shift. You dozed off."

"Wow." I looked at my watch, 11:45pm "Thanks, dear." *Dear? I don't talk that way.* I looked at her face and saw no reaction.

I got up, stretched and said, "Ok, I've got the helm. Slaap lekker." I just loved the Dutch expression meaning have a delicious sleep.

Yvonne came over to me, gave my shoulder a squeeze and said, "Danke, lieve Boots" and went below.

They were seated in the *Raptor's* salon drinking coffee. They had had a quiet breakfast at Bonnie's, after which they had used the zodiac that was tied up at the small dock by Bonnie's to motor out to the *Raptor*.

"So, Eagle, how do we find the boats to steal," asked Owl, putting down his coffee cup.

They all looked at Eagle who said, "That is for me to worry about. Suffice it to say I will get the information, send Falcon and Buzz out on the sub to get the boat and your job, Owl, along with Hawk will be to take the newly acquired boats south to Antigua to sell. There are always buyers on Antigua."

"What sub?" asked Falcon.

"I bought a two person sub that I found on Craig's list. It is tied up alongside us right now," said Eagle. "You'll see it soon enough. Are you all ready for your first assignment?"

Falcon, Hawk and Owl looked at Eagle with a smile and nodded.

Buzzard nodded without looking at Eagle.

"So, here is the set up. A young couple on their honeymoon is in their boat which is tied up in Princess Bay, a cove on the north side of Hurricane Hole at the east end of St. John. Falcon and Buzzard will take the sub to Tutu Bay and wait until night. When night arrives, they will board their boat, *Serendipity*, do what needs to be done and bring Serendipity here. Hawk and Owl will then sail it to Antigua, sell it and fly back here. Any questions?"

"Yes. What do you mean, do what has to be done?" asked Buzzard.

"It means removed, eliminated, killed," said Eagle in a growling voice.

"I don't want any part of any killing," said, Buzz.

"I told you in the beginning," said Eagle, "that there would be no turning back."

"But… but I didn't know there would be any killing," said Buzz.

"Too bad, Buzz. You can only leave two ways," said Falcon, "with us when we stop or, take a swim wearing lead ankle bracelets."

Buzz shrunk back in her seat, visibly shaking.

"Falcon and Buzz, you leave in the morning," said Eagle.

"I won't do it, I won't" said Buzz.

"You most certainly will," said Eagle. "This is my show. Don't ever forget it."

Buzz sat silently, tears rolling down her cheeks.

"I'll never get in her pants now," thought Eagle, raging inside.

Chapter Sixteen

We had settled into our routine well and the next three days passed with no incident. The morning of day four found us northwest of Isla de Culebra, about 30 miles from the East End of St. Thomas. Red had told me that the Elysian Beach Club had a place to tie up for free, and that the American Yacht Club in Redhook has a full service marina. I wanted to tie up in one of those places as the East End was where the life jacket was found and not far from where the body was found. I opted for the marina since we needed fuel, water and groceries. Also, it seemed that we'd be just one of the other tourists if we were in a marina.

The winter months can be cold in the Bahamas and I remember a February with evening temperatures down to 43°. Now being so much further south, the temperature during the day was getting into the 80s and the humidity was rising. I felt the morning sun heating up the boat. Thankfully, we had a good breeze to cool us off as long as we kept moving and the hatches open and I could turn on the air-conditioning if necessary.

Cappy who had kept on the 4am to 8am shift, came down to the galley where I was having my morning brew. Yvonne had relieved him at the helm.

"Yo, Good morning."

"Yo yourself, you old shrink you," I responded with a wink.

"Shrink, shrank, shrunk. Thanks, pal. I'm going to go below and get some much needed sleep."

"Okey dokey Cap, rest well. We'll have a planning session at lunch."
"I will do that, Boots, see you at noon."

I went up to the bridge where the breeze was moist from the choppy sea. "A fresh cup of brew for the helmsperson," and handed the coffee to Yvonne.

"Thanks mate, and how are you this morning?"

I took the seat next to her and said, "I feel wonderful, Vonnie." I wanted to say 'because you are with me' but I held back and I didn't know why. I needed a talk with our resident shrink.

"That's good to hear. I feel wonderful too. Boots, when I look over the side, the water is so clear, sometimes I see sharks and huge sea turtles and other fish I can't identify. The sharks scare me, Boots."

"They are scary to me too, very. Believe me, I avoid them. The sea turtles are fascinating to watch for sure. So big and so graceful. By the way, I told Cappy that we'd have a planning session at noon," and leaned back watching her do her turn at the helm.

I checked our nav chart. "Yvonne, We'll stay on 95° until we are south of Charlotte Amalie, about an hour from now then switch to 73°. Until lunch. Okay by you?"

"How will I know when we are there?"

"You'll see all the cruise ships lined up, Vonnie. I'm going to check my email. I'll be up in a bit," I said, as I gave her a light caress on her shoulder. Just as I turned away, I saw her give me a quizzical look. Well, that makes two of us who are confuzzled.

I went below and through the salon and down to my office. I was always logged in, though Cappy told me it was not a good idea. I had a bunch of emails, all but two marked as spam. One was from Julie asking how we were progressing so I sent a quick note filling her in. The other was from Red. "Boots, the FBI and Coast Guard had pooled their info. All the boats had at least one female. All the females were under 35 and all of them were blonde. I hope all is well, 'R'" Shit. Blast it all, Yvonne is 32 and blonde. I need to talk to Cappy.

I went up to the salon, knowing Cappy would be there. "Good morning, Boots. How you be?" he said in between sips of his black, unsweetened coffee. Yeck.

"I'm not so sure, Cap, not sure at all," and I told him about Red's email."

"We sure have a problem, my friend. We need to proceed slowly and carefully and be very very aware of everything that goes on around us. Tying up in Redhook seems to be the smart thing to do. Then I think we need to do some casual detective work"

"We?"

"Well, you and me, friend, surely not Yvonne."

"Since when did you become a detective, you old shrink person?"

"Since listening to your exploits, fool."

"Ok, ok, in a limited fashion. What I want is to find out if any of the locals are aware of any new faces that have been around the last six months. Faces that don't seem to be employed. Can you go be your sociable shrink kind of self at the local marinas and places that serve the marinas?"

"Yes, sir, sir."

"Cap?"

"Yes, Boots?"

"Why can't I tell Vonnie that I love her?"

"Do you?"

"Do I what?"

"Love her, silly?"

"Yes, I do."

"Then, ask out loud in your head, 'Why can't I tell Vonnie I love her'. Listen for the answer and write it down on paper and bring it to me."

"Talk in my head?"

"Yes, in your head"

"Ok, I'll try it but., one of us is crazy."

Chapter Seventeen

The autopilot was quietly doing its thing as we relaxed on the fantail, having a glass of wine when I noticed whitecaps were stirred up and I had a hunch I better check "weatherbug" for the local forecast. My laptop was just inside the wheelhouse on the chart table so I took a peek. Sure enough there was an alert for a thunderstorm between 6 and 8pm.

We were about a half hour sail from Great Bay where we would have to change course to go northwest to Redhook. If we altered course now from our present 68° to 114°, we could tie up between Great St. James Island and on Little St. James. There was a tiny cove on the north side of Little St. James that would be perfect. I altered course on the autopilot and went back outside to the fantail.

"There is a storm coming so I've altered course to get us into a cove for shelter."

Yvonne and Cappy, engrossed in a conversation, seemed unaware that I had spoken.

"Hey you two, I just saw an elephant float by."

"Uh huh," said Cappy. Yvonne looked at me, smiled and went back to talking to Cappy.

Well, ok, I'll just sit at the helm and act like a skipper. The wind out of the northeast was getting stronger and the skies were getting darker. I swiveled around and raised my voice to be heard above the ever increasing volume of the wind.

"Yo. Cap, Vonnie. We need to anchor in a cove that will appear on the starboard in about 10 minutes. Cap, get the bow anchor ready, Vonnie, get the stern anchor ready to drop."

"Aye aye, skipper," came the almost simultaneous response as they got up and brought their wine glasses inside. Vonnie came back and got the anchor from under the fantail settee. I could see Cappy up front, anchor at his feet, ready to throw. I started the engines and put them in forward gear with the throttle set at a very slow speed. I flipped the switches to reef the sails and when they were all secure, I slowed down even more as we approached the center of the cove. The nav chart said we had 20 feet but I wanted to play safe. I put the engines in reverse for a count of 5, then neutral.

"Throw it Cap," I shouted.

I put us in reverse and very slowly backed up.

"Enough," shouted Cap when he saw the anchor line start to tighten up. I put us in forward gear for a count of 5 and then to neutral.

"Drop yours, Vonnie," I said over my shoulder. As soon as I heard the kerplop, I put us in forward.

"She's tightening up, Boots," came the word from Yvonne. I immediately put us in neutral and turned off the engine, knowing our anchors were set and that we could ride out the storm.

To our west, I could see the wall of rain about a thousand yards away and I could hear the wind howling along with occasional claps of thunder.   "We'd better get below."

We went into the salon. Cappy and I sat on the swivel chairs and Yvonne went into the galley.

"How about soup for lunch, guys?"

"Good with me," said Cappy.

"Me too." I listened to the rain pounding on the deck, interrupted by a clap of thunder that seemed to shake the boat as lightning lit up the inside of the lounge. Yvonne was cheffing in the galley when she said, "Boots, are we safe?"

"Yes, Vonnie, we are as long as we stay inside. I promise."

"From your mouth to God's ears, ole buddy." Cappy said. Cappy and I sat in the swivel chairs, both of us listening to the singing of the wind and steady drumbeat of the rain on the overhead deck

"Okay guys, soup is on the pass-through. Help yourselves."

We served ourselves soup and the garlic bread Yvonne had made and settled at the table to eat.

"In the morning, we will motor over to Redhook and tie up at the marina. It's about 4 miles so about an hour, given we need to go slow for most of the trip. We hook into shore side services, have lunch and then we begin our work.

"So, our agenda… Cappy, will you go chat up the locals, Yvonne and I will go visit the local police to check in. I don't want Yvonne to be alone on the boat."

"Okay by me, Boots."

"Anything you say dear." *Dear?* I gave Yvonne a smile. I need to do what Cappy asked me to do. I need to make time to do that.

Chapter Eighteen

I was in my office checking my email. Nada. My desktop computer was built in to cabinetry I'd had installed in the starboard cabin, forward of the lounge. The computer was surrounded by foam to absorb the shocks of being in a boat. When I'd bought the boat, I'd had the bunks removed from that cabin and in their place I'd built a wall of cabinetry with a pull down desk and sliding drawer for the keyboard. My flat screen monitor was in the back of the desk, directly below the porthole. Because I am fussy about such things, I was tweaking the color values.

My cell phone rang once and stopped before I had a chance to answer. The screen said missed call. *Blasted phone company.* This was a common problem but at least I had the phone number of the caller and it was Red. I clicked Send and it automatically dialed his number.

"Yo, Red. You rang?"

"Yes, can you talk?

"Sure, what's up?"

"Some kids over at the Ritz-Carlton found a piece of another lifejacket washed up on the beach, same as the last one. They took it to their mom and she called the police who called us. This one had a 'Y' stenciled on it."

"Thanks, Red. I think we are in the right place to be working on this."

"Be careful."

"Yup." I hung up and got the chart out. From the chart, I knew that the Ritz Carlton beach was between the Elysian Beach Hotel and Redhook. I sat back to think.

I must have fallen asleep. I was dreaming of being chased by a shark in a dark alley. The shark had on roller skates. Huge jaws snapping at my heels as I ran. I woke up and there was a thunderous noise that came from a jetliner passing overhead. The sound of it was deafening. I ran topside as fast as I could watched helplessly as a jumbo jet smashed nose first into the water so violently, the tail section snapped off as if it were made of balsa wood. My head was fuzzy, as I watched in disbelief. It is too difficult for my brain to compute. I suddenly realized I'd woken up from one nightmare to the reality of another. Julie, Yvonne, I screamed, where are you both? But that didn't make sense. I had to do something, but what could I do? I shook my head and my eyes opened up. *Holy shit, I had a dream within a dream.* I was drenched in sweat, heart racing, feeling afraid. I remembered something Cappy taught me to do when panicked. I looked around the cabin. At the walls, deck, overhead. I saw no danger. Out loud in my head I said, 'Relax. Nothing is happening now. I know it feels like it but I just checked and we are ok. Relax' I felt almost instantly better.

The rain was still coming down but not as hard as I went up the few steps aft to the salon.

"Hey Cap, where's Yvonne?"

"She went to take a nap."

"Cap, I had a weird dream."

"Tell me, Boots." Cappy loved dreams.

"I dreamed I was in dark alley in some city being chased by a shark on roller skates. He was snapping at my heels when all of a sudden I was back on Grand Abaco, witnessing that jetliner crash that Yvonne somehow survived. Then I woke up in a panic and did our anti-panic routine."

"Did it work?"

"Duh."

Cappy smiled and said, "So?"

"What's with the 'So' again?"

"You know it's one of my favorite words, besides, you told *me* about the dream, So?"

"Good grief. You are impossible. Cappy was nodding his head and smiling.

"The dreams scared me, Cappy. Terrified me, actually. What do they mean? A dream within a dream. Give me a break."

"Look, Boots, we are doing something very dangerous."

"Your shark dream suggests that you believe we have the two-legged kind involved in these disappearances. The jet crash suggests worry about Yvonne. Both dreams suggest that we are all in danger. I think you are correct. I think we need to be very careful. We need to be on high alert at all times."

"Hey guys what's up?" asked Yvonne rubbing her eyes as she came up into the salon?

"What's up is what's for dinner?" said, Cappy

"Chauvinist." said, Yvonne.

Chapter Nineteen

We'd shared another of Yvonne's gourmet meals… Caesar salad and baked salmon filets coated with almonds, breadcrumbs, dill served with a dill and mustard sauce. A nice white zinfandel complimented the meal.

We'd not spoken of our purpose here, only the things we'd like to do vacation-wise here on St. Thomas and on St. John, supposedly the location of the most beautiful beaches in the world. We turned in early, partly from a bit too much wine and partly because we were all exhausted.

With the wind howling and the rain pounding on deck above, Yvonne and I lay in each other's arms, the boat rocking us to sleep. As I drifted off I wondered if I had bitten off more than I could chew. I wondered…

All of a sudden I was in the water, waves breaking over my head, Yvonne in front of me, yelling for help. I swam towards her but the wind was pushing her away just as fast. "Hang on, Vonnie, hang on," I yelled over the sound of the wind. She went under and I couldn't find her. "No, Vonnie, No, you cannot die. No." I screamed.

Yvonne shook me, "Boots, wake up."

"Huh? Wha?" I shook my head and sat up. "Are you ok? What's going on?" I was totally disoriented.

"Yes, I am ok. You were having a bad dream, lieve Boots. I am ok, really."

"My God, I thought I lost you, Vonnie I…"

"You what, Boots? What were you trying to say?"

"I don't know, Vonnie. I'm not awake yet." But I did know. I almost said, 'I love you, Vonnie." I need to do that homework Cappy gave me.

We shared a shower, almost got delayed by helping each other use the soap but decided we would play later. Yvonne put on some blue shorts with a white blouse sprinkled with polka dots and tennis shoes. I put on denim cut-offs with a Club Med Eleuthera T-shirt and boat shoes.

We went up to the salon where we found Cappy.

"Breakfast is served you two. Have a seat and I, your server for *this* meal, will bring your food to you."

And he did. He brought us coffee, OJ, bacon, English muffins and scrambled eggs. He brought enough for himself and sat with us.

"So?"

"So what? Cappy," I said. "Is this a shrink question? A friendly question? I trick question?"

"Just a normal 'So'," Boots.

"Oh boy. Ok. I am a bit edgy about what we are doing. I have a bad feeling in my gut that says we need to be extra extra careful. So as they say on the television, 'If you see something, say something, no matter how silly it may be, say it.' Ok you two?"

"Yes, Boots," Cappy said.

"Ok, but it seems like you want me to have back of the head eyes, Boots."

Cappy and I both grinned. "You mean, eyes in back of your head," Vonnie, right?"

"Yes, that, Boots."

"All right then. We will raise anchor, sail almost due north, past Great St. James Island, northwest to Great Bay where we will follow its contour slowly counter-clockwise until we are on a heading of 240° which will take us into the Redhook harbor. The American Yacht Club will be to starboard. Any questions?"

"Yeah, where can I get a lobster?" Cappy asked.

"Keep a sharp eye on the water, Cappy, you never know." I looked at Yvonne and Cappy and said, "Cap, forward to the anchor line, Yvonne, aft to yours."

They both nodded and we all went topside. I started the engine, reversed slowly until Yvonne could raise her anchor, went immediately to forward gear and went slowly until Cappy could raise his anchor. I kept us under way only to keep us from drifting until they both had their anchors stowed, then forward at normal cruising speed. Cappy and Yvonne came and sat with me on the bridge. It was a beautiful day, temperature about 78° with a refreshing, gentle breeze from the west. There were seagulls and the occasional pelican diving for a meal as we rounded Great St. James and headed northwest towards St. Thomas-Redhook Bay.

A freighter made its way south. To Venezuela perhaps. I often fantasized about the destinations of boats and cars that I saw. There were plenty to pick from... water skiers, parasailors, ferry boats, passenger liners, powerboats, sailboats and motorsailors like this one going from here to there and back again. Another parasailor came into view and visions of Sandy falling to her death came flooding into my mind and I shuddered.

"Boots?"

"Huh? Vonnie? What?" I said as I shook my head.

"You looked like you were far off and hurting," Yvonne said with a concerned look on her face.

"Can I tell you later? I think I need to concentrate on navigating."

"You will tell me later. I have mind like iron trap," said Yvonne, tapping her forehead.

"Yes, I bet I will," I said giving her a wink. We were coming abeam of the channel so I swung almost due west to 256° and with less than a mile to go, slowed to 4 knots.

"Cappy and Yvonne, keep a sharp lookout for water-skiers. I'm going to go past the marina and turn in a 180 so that we are facing out of the harbor when we tie up."

"Aye aye, Boots," came the almost simultaneous responses.

I made a sharp turn to starboard and slowed to a crawl, just fast enough to have control.

"Cappy, forward, Yvonne aft. Be ready to tie on to the dock."

I edged to port and pulled along the outside of the 1st T-dock I came to, reversed the engines until we were stopped, then went to neutral.

"Now, Cap and Yvonne."

I watched them both jump onto the dock and make their lines fast to the cleats and then turned off the engines as they came back to the bridge.

"Well done, mates."

"I need to go to the harbormaster and register us. When I come back, customs will inspect our boat and our passports. In the meantime, how about making sure the kitties have food and water and relax. After customs, we'll lock up and sit outside at Molly's for lunch, my treat to my crew. Okay?"

I saw big smiles, heard no words as I walked down the gangplank towards the office of American Yacht Harbor.

Chapter Twenty

We were seated dockside, under an umbrella, at Molly Malone's Pub, drinking beer and enjoying hamburgers and fries when Yvonne said, "So?" There was a nice breeze coming off the water, keeping us comfortable.

"So what?" I said deadpan but I knew.

Cappy looked first at Yvonne, then at me, then chimed in with, "Yeah, So?"

"Oh boy. A conspiracy."

"You promised, Boots, you did. He did, Cappy, honest."

I did not want to talk about it but I knew I probably should. Besides, Cappy would bug me knowing there was something going on. I took a long pull at my beer, finishing the stein and signaling for another

"Ok, ok." I took a deep breath. "Years ago, when I worked in New York City, I was friendly with a young woman named Sandy. Sandy worked in the office across the hall from my office and we'd chat from time to time. Had coffee but never a date. One day when I came in, as I was turning the key in my lock, her office manager happened to be coming out of their office. She greeted me by name and said, 'Hey did you read about Sandy?'"

My gut tightened as I said, 'Read about Sandy where?'

'In the Herald Tribune, she was sky diving and her chute didn't open'.

Tears are now streaming down my face and Yvonne takes my hand under the table and holds it tight.

"'Strange thing,' Sandy's office manager added. 'Her desk was clean for the first time ever, like she didn't expect to come back.' With that, she walked down the corridor to the elevators without looking back."

"I've been haunted ever since, wondering what it was like for her in those final moments after the chute didn't open, knowing she was going to die."

"I never cried until now, twenty-five years later." I grabbed a napkin and wiped my eyes.

"I'm sorry, lieve Boots," said Yvonne squeezing my hand even tighter.

"Boots, I'm sorry you lost her. I'm glad you finally were able to talk about it. I know it must hurt like hell."

"Thanks, you two. I'm glad too. Hell of a way to celebrate our arrival on St. Thomas.

I'd not paid any attention to our surroundings until now but I had a slight tingling in my shoulders that needed attention. I'd been facing the *Lost & Found,* Cappy on my right, Yvonne on my left at a circular table.

"Yvonne, when I say 'go', do me a favor and go up and ask the bartender where the best shops in Redhook are for you to buy resort clothes."

"Cappy, I have the tingle alert which usually means that someone is paying attention to me so, when Yvonne gets up, turn and watch her walk but keep your antennae on. I'm going to do the same to see if I can figure out who it is."

"Yvonne, 'go.'" Yvonne got up and walked to the bar.

Cappy and I turned and watched her. So did eyes of all the other men except one. Cap, take a quick look at nine o'clock as you turn back around.

"The tall one with blue and yellow shirt?" asked Cappy as he turned towards me with his eyes on Yvonne as she wove her way between the tables on her return.

"That's the one, Cap."

"Thanks, Vonnie, you did great."

"What did I do, Boots, I'm confuzzled."

"You fine-tuned my internal radar, Vonnie. We have some unusual interest in me or us that I need to figure out. Memorize the face of the tall one with blue and yellow shirt at the table two over to our left. Wait until we get up before you look."

I signaled for the waiter to bring the bill.

I paid the tab and got up slowly using my peripheral vision to check him out without ever making eye contact. Yvonne and Cappy followed me to the boat, my back registering the following eyes of the man in stripes.

Chapter Twenty-One

We were back on board, seated in the lounge, Pietje and Stafje seated on the back of the couch, staring out the windows at the gulls diving for food in the wake of passing boats.

"I need to check in with Carl Ricci, Red's FBI friend. How about you two go for a walk and keep an eye out for the one who was staring, ok? I want to know if you are followed. But, stay in crowds, please. Do not go where there are no other people."

"Okay, Boots," said Cappy with a smile. "Yvonne and I will go have some touristy fun." And off they went.

My cell phone rang and as I grabbed it, it stopped. Then I heard a two tone chime and a notice on the screen read, 'missed call.'
Blasted Verizon. Give me a chance, eh? I *86ed to listen to my messages. Only one and it was from Julie in New York. "Boots, be careful. My gut says you are in danger. Love ya."

My instincts and her guts means I better be extra careful. Julie was never wrong. I dialed Carl Ricci's number. He answered on the first ring.

"This is Carl."

"Carl, my name is Boots Beaumont, a friend of Red Baron and he gave me your number. I'm in St. Thomas now sitting at Molly Malone's in Redhook. Have a minute?"

"Boots, how do I know you are a friend of Red's?"

"Well, we worked together on those plane crashes that turned out to be sabotage and he helped me break up a black-market baby ring."

"Okay then, for a friend of Red's what's it about?"

"I'd rather not discuss it on the phone. Can we meet?"

"Sure, but not at Molly's. I'll meet you at Duffy's Love Shack in 10 minutes. It's across the street and down a bit from Molly's and sort of in the parking lot of a strip mall. How will I recognize you?"

"I'm wearing cut-offs and a Club Med Eleuthera T-shirt. How will I kn…"

"Worry not, I'll find you, Boots." And he abruptly hung up.

I closed my cell phone and Julie's warning popping back into my head.

Chapter Twenty-Two

I walked up the gangplank to the dock finger and walked up to Smith Bay Road and over to Molly Malone's. The breeze was gentle and enjoyable. The streets were busy. I said hello to a few locals which was a polite and almost mandatory custom on St. Thomas. For some reason, other than the locals, I only noticed the women who were clad in shorts and halter tops. *Hmm, I'll have to ask Cappy about that.* For some reason most of them were in pairs, chirping away and smiling but I didn't think that was what Cappy would say was the reason. I looked across the street and saw the strip mall and Duffy's.

By now it was mid-afternoon and the heat of the tropical sun was brutal as I crossed the street. I could feel my exposed skin sizzling. I went to the entrance and asked for an outside table for two and was seated in an uncomfortable chair. Then again, so were most restaurant chairs. *Another question for Cappy?* Aside from the restaurant proper, which held perhaps ten tables, there were about 30 tables spread out in the parking. About half were full. As I looked around to get my bearings, someone sat down across from me. He was about six foot tall, stocky with sun-bleached hair and wearing blue jeans with a pale blue Izod sport shirt.

"Mr. Beaumont, now that we are seated together, me with a gun pointed at you under the table, just to be doubly sure, since you could have read about the planes and baby selling in the papers, what is Red's legal first name?"

"Wow, sure... his legal 1st name is Frank and his nickname was given to him in Quantico. You sure are edgy."

I could see the tension disappear from his face as he smiled and held his hand out to shake.

"No hard feelings."

I shook his hand and said, "None."

Just then the waiter, clad in some kind of pirate outfit complete with an eye patch, appeared and said, "Gentlemen?"

Without looking Carl said, "Well, I've not had lunch so I'll have a *windward* burger medium rare."

The waiter looked at me with a raised eyebrow on the unpatched eye.

"Just an iced tea for me."

The waiter lowered his eyebrow, scowled and walked away.

"You hurt his feelings, Boots."

"I will repent, Carl. Really I will," I said with a smile.

"So, what brings you to St. Thomas and why did Red refer you to me?"

"You know about the lifejacket found at the Ritz-Carlton and the girl's body found on Great St. James?

"Yes, I'm aware of that investigation. What is your interest in it?"

I told him how I got involved from the beginning bringing him up-to-date.

Carl said, "I had no idea about the enormity of this case, Boots. I had no way of knowing until now. However I think I have some information that can help you. I can tell you it's the birds

"*For* the birds?"

Just then the waiter appeared, his tray balanced in his left hand, serving us with his right. "Enjoy, gentlemen."

Carl picked up his burger to take a bite, "Yes, bir.."

The waiter started to turn and walk away.

Suddenly there was a splash of red on the waiter's shirt and face. I thought for one moment that it was catsup until I saw that Carl's head wasn't there anymore. It had exploded. Blood and bits of his head and face were everywhere, on me, the table, the waiter and those at nearby tables. Carl had been turned off.

Chapter Twenty-Three

I was stone cold, in spite of the heat. I had flattened out on the pavement and stayed put until I was sure there was not going to be any more shooting. There was a lot of screaming and frantic running all around me. I started to get up but my hands slipped on the blood on the pavement. I rolled to the side and wiped my hands against my cut-offs and got up.

Carl's body was lying on the table, minus most of his head. As I looked at his bloody, destroyed body, I realized that I never heard the sound of the shot that killed him but I knew it had to be a high powered rifle. I looked around and saw that a crowd had gathered at a distance, people gawking. I wonder what makes people want to stare at blood and guts. Maybe just thanking God it was not them. A police car had pulled into the parking lot and I saw three of St. Thomas' finest walking towards me rather briskly as I was righting my tipped over chair.

"Sir, are you hurt?" asked the cop with the sergeant's stripes.

I sat down and said, "Not that I know of, Officer."

An ambulance pulled in and two EMTs popped out and started to run to Carl, saw that he had no head and almost stopped dead in their tracks, faces aghast at the horror.

"What happened here?" asked the sergeant."

"We were just served lunch when his head exploded. I heard no sound of a weapon being fired. I jumped under the table in terror." That was an understatement.

He asked me for I.D and where I was staying. While he and I were talking, one of the other cops was going through Carl's wallet looking for his I.D. and said, "Sarg, this guy's FBI."

"Why were you talking to an FBI man, Mr. Beaumont?" asked the sergeant.

"We have a mutual friend in the states so I thought I'd look him up, Sergeant."

"Do you have any idea why someone would want to kill him?"

"No sir, we had just met. I'm clueless and shaking in my boots," and I was shaking in my boots." Cappy would love this sentence for sure.

"Mr. Beaumont, you can go for now but do not leave St. Thomas. I presume we can contact you at the marina?"

"Yes, sir, you can and I will not leave." I got up on shaky legs and started to walk away. I saw the sergeant nod to the cop who had been standing on the side, keeping the crowd back.

"Mr. Beaumont, would you like a ride to the marina?"

"Yes, I would, sir."

"Hop in front with me," said the cop.

"Are you enjoying your stay on our beautiful island, sir?" he said?

"Well, I was, but now…"

"I understand sir. I'm sorry you lost your friend." I became aware that he was watching my face very closely as well as paying attention to the road.

"So am I." I looked at him directly before putting my head down. I was still shaking and it showed. I rubbed my eyes with my hands, shook my head. "Very much so."

We pulled into the American Yacht Club lot and asked, "Are you ok?"

"I will be after I have time to unwind. Thank you for your courtesy officer."

"Don't mention it sir."

I got out of the police car and walked towards the *Lost & Found.*

I was still shaky and took my time walking, oblivious to all around me. As soon as I got on board, I sat down in the lounge and opened my cell phone. It had dried blood on it, so I wiped that off and then wiped the whole phone with sanitizer.

Then I dialed, waited, and spoke. "Red, we need to talk."

From the Eagle Chronicles # 8

"Approaching St. James Island, 15 minutes out. Buzzard and Falcon, over," said Buzz.

"Come north into Cowpet Bay, then bear ENE until you see *Raptor*. Pull along the starboard side. Keep Sub on starboard side of *Tayana*," said Eagle.

"Roger. Over and out," said Buzz.

"Son of a bitch, fucking son of a bitch," Buzz said out loud. " How did I get myself into this mess."

Buzzard was alone in the Sub, riding just under the surface, Falcon following in the *Tayana*. She remembered being told that she couldn't back out. Eagle had made a remark about how deep and dark the water was in Cowpet Bay. His eyes had bored into her when he said it. She remembered that the others were looking at her as well, watching for her reaction, especially Falcon. She could almost smell his rage, his lust for blood and it scared her.

I remember when he came aboard after killing the family on Tayana and there was some dried blood on his upper lip. It made me start to wonder if he…

She started to hum to herself to stop the thoughts. Mindless humming. We are almost there.

"We have *Raptor* in sight. Buzzard and Falcon, over."

"Roger," said Eagle, "pull *Tayana* along my starboard side, Sub on her starboard side. Buzz swim to my starboard side ladder. Do not be seen."

Click click was heard from Falcon's radio.

"Roger that," said Buzz.

Chapter Twenty-Four

"What's going on, Boots? Are you ok?"

"Yeah, I'm just ducky but Carl Ricci was killed this morning."

"What?"

"Yes, he was shot in the head while we were at an outdoor restaurant. We had just met and his head exploded in front of me."

"OMG, Boots. I need to get right on this. Where are you?"

"I'm on my boat now, the local fuzz brought me back from the restaurant."

"I need to go through his reports. I need to get an undercover replacement sent down ASAP. I need to talk to my supervisor, I need a drink. Be very careful, Boots. I'll get back to you."

I was exhausted so I checked on the cats, grabbed a beer out of the fridge and went on the afterdeck to stretch out on one of the mats to relax.

All of a sudden, out of the corner of my eye I saw a jet, coming in low over the water, heading straight for the marina. The engines were screaming loudly but the plane was coming lower, right towards me, I was frozen, unable to move, I could see the pilot in the cockpit window just before…

"Boots, yo, Boots? Wake up."

I opened my eyes. "Huh? Cappy, Vonnie? Are you ok?" I looked at them, then at the boat. "Wow, I was back at the plane crash in the Bahamas nightmare."

"You ok, Boots?" asked Vonnie as she came next to me and put her hand on my cheek.

"Ok enough. Can you two sit for a moment? Maybe grab a beer first?" They both looked at me in a funny way, went in and came back rather quickly with beer bottles in their hands, standing there staring at me strangely.

"Why are you two looking at me that way?"

"Well you are normally a neat eater but you have catsup splotches on your clothes, my friend."

I realized I had not showered or changed clothes since I came back. "It's not catsup. Take a seat and I'll explain."

They sat and I told them what had occurred.

"My God, Boots, You are lucky to be alive." said, Cappy.

"I don't think whoever it was intended to kill me."

"I don't hope so too," said, Yvonne.

"They had ample time to fire a second shot and didn't. I think Carl was the intended target."

Cappy said, "From what you've told me, I have to agree. But then the question arises. Does this have anything to do with the missing girls?"

"Only time will tell. Meanwhile, did you and Yvonne find anything out?"

"No, no exactly. We were followed," said, Yvonne. We walked from one end of Smith Bay Road to the other, stopping here and there to look in shops. Striped shirt was never far away and then all of a sudden he was gone."

"He was very good, Boots. If I hadn't been looking to see if someone was following us, I'd not have noticed him."

Yvonne said, "Me too."

I smiled at Yvonne, winked at Cappy and said, "I'm going to take a shower. How about you two figure out where you'd like to go for dinner.

Chapter Twenty-Five

When I got out of the shower and dressed, I found Cappy and Yvonne in the lounge, each with a cat on their lap. They were smiling and I could swear the cats were too.

"So?"

"What?" said Cappy and Yvonne almost simultaneously.

"Dinner is what."

"What about dinner?" asked Cappy

"Oh boy. This is like pulling teeth."

"You like going to the dentist?" asked Yvonne in amazement.

"No, Yvonne, It's an American expression. He means he is struggling to get us to tell him that we are going to Bonnie's by the Sea for dinner."

"Oh, I see. I mean I don't see but ok, let's eat. Ik hap hawnger," she said with a big grin on her face.

"Okay, you are hungry, Vonnie. Let's go hail a cab you two," I said and walked to the cabin door, knowing they would follow.

We walked down the dock. The salt air had a pleasant hint of bougainvillea. The ringing of the halyards was mixed with sounds of the water lapping against the hulls of the yachts we passed. At Smith Bay Road and we got into one of the waiting taxis.

"Where to?" said the lady driver, "My name is Gwyneth."

I said, "Gwyneth, do you know where Bonnie's by the sea is?"
"Everyone knows Bonnie's, said Gwyneth turning to look back over her shoulder before putting the taxi in gear and making a U-turn to head west on Smith Bay Road.

Yvonne started pulling on my arm frantically. "Boots, Boots, she is driving on the wrong side of the road, she will get us killed. Stop her, Boots."

"Yvonne, on this island and some others in the Caribbean, they drive on the other side of the road."

"Danke, I mean thanks, phew, wow." said Yvonne as she slumped against me.

I gave took her hand and smiled as the cab went up the hill to the Elysian Beach resort and then down their steep driveway where she let us off.

"Ten dollars please sir," said Gwyneth. "Bonnies is off to the left."

"Thank you, Gwyneth, here is twelve," I said.

"Thank YOU Sir." said Gwyneth.

As we got out of the cab, I looked around at the surroundings. I wanted to know how to leave if we had a problem. I heard Gwyneth drive off as I turned away from her car. Behind me, on the hill I could see several hotel buildings spread out and climbing up, each floor slightly back from the one below. There was a tennis court between us and the hill. Further to my left was a swimming pool.

"Boots?"

"One more minute, Vonnie," I said. "I'm just doing some prep work."

Turning back around, in front of me and slightly to the right was the beach with a marina with boats moored in a haphazard fashion. No docks, no office. Slightly to the left, past the curve of the beach, I could see a dozen or so round tables with beach umbrellas spread out in front of a bar with a few patrons sitting on stools.

I pointed and said, "Looks like Bonnie's is that way."

There were sounds of crickets and palm fronds moving in a gentle breeze. "Prep for what, Boots," asked Bonnie.

"He's looking for ways to get out of here if we are in trouble, Yvonne. It's a good habit," said Cappy. "And Boots, how did you hear about this very out of the way place?"

"I asked the harbormaster for something out of the way and…well, this is it."

We walked to someone who seemed to work there and I said, 'three please."

"Follow me if you will." She led us to a table near the water. "Denis will be with you shortly." She smiled, handed us menus and left us. We sat down, Yvonne between Cappy and myself. Cappy looked up and seemed to be checking the sky above us.

Just past the bay, the sun was dipping below the horizon, the sky turning golden, the air pleasantly warm.

All of a sudden Yvonne grabbed my hand and screamed, "Look.".

Chapter Twenty-Six

I looked in the direction she was looking and saw two rather large iguanas walking across the sand close to our table.

"Yvonne, those are iguanas, they are everywhere on St. Thomas. If you don't bother them, they won't bother you."

"You promise?"

"Yes, I promise."

"One thing about them," said Cappy, "they sleep in the leaves at the top of the palm trees and sometimes they fall while they're sleeping. I made sure we were in the open so we don't have to worry about one falling on our table. I checked as we sat down."

"Good griefs," said, Yvonne/ "I'm glad we don't have to have worry."

"Me too."

"Me three," said Cappy.

We looked at our menus.

A dignified looking gentleman with a warm smile came to our table. "My name is Denis. Would you like to order drinks and hear the specials?"

"I'd like a rum hit," said Yvonne. Denis looked at her with a raised eyebrow. Yvonne looked puzzled.

"She means a rum punch," I said, and I'll have the same.

"Please make that three, Denis," said Cappy.

"Thank you. The special entrees this evening are broiled fresh sea bass with Bonnie's special salsa and 1-1/2 pound boiled lobster. I'll be right back with your drinks."

"So," said Cappy, "Why are we on this island?"

"We have nowhere to go except here. I think as we move around we are stirring the pot. Striped shirt must know we have some connection to the FBI. Else, why would he be following you?"

Cappy nodded with a frown.

Yvonne was eyeing the iguanas.

"Cappy, where could they be hiding the boats?"

"It's obvious, Boots, They are hiding them in plain sight."

Cappy says, "Look at all the boats in this Marina. No one checks them. Look at the one's further out in Cowpet bay. They are effectively invisible. Let's bring the *Lost & Found* over here and look around or rent a small boat and putter around the bay?"

"I think that's a goo.." I stopped in mid-sentence as over Cappy's shoulder I saw striped shirt with three other men and a woman sit down two tables away. "Cappy and Yvonne, do not look around but striped shirt is here with four others at a table behind Cappy. Striped shirt is looking our way so let's just concentrate on our dinner choices. "

"Boots, I need to use the rest room. I noticed where it is, so excuse me," said Cappy who got up, turned and walked past the table of five.

"Boots, I don't like this."

"Neither do I, Vonnie, neither do I." I took her hand. "Let's try to enjoy our dinner. I'll keep us all safe." I meant it and I hoped I could keep the promise.

Cappy returned at the same time Denis came back to our table with our drinks.

Before he could say a word, Yvonne held up the unlit candle from our table and said to Denis, "Loosie Fair?"

 Denis looked at Yvonne, then at me, then at Cappy with a quizzical smile. "Do you want me to light the candle, Miss?"

Yes, "Loosie fair."

Denis shook his head, lit the candle and then placed our drinks in front of us, and with a big grin said, "Three rum hits. Have you decided on your main course?"

Yvonne said, "I'd like the sea bass please."

"Same for me," said Cappy.

"Make that three, Denis."

Denis smiled and said, "you three are delightfully easy to serve."

"Ok, ok. What's with the Loosie Fair?" I said.

"What don't you understand, Boots?" said, Yvonne. Asking someones if they would light something or wants a light, you use the devils name with a question at end of the sentence. What is hard to get, huh?"

"Omg, she means Lucifer," said Cappy.

"That's what I said, silly mens, Loosie Fair."

Yvonne, when speaking English, we say, 'Lucifer' in 3 syllables said rapidly as one word. 'Lucifer'. You try

"Loosie Fair." said Yvonne with a grin.

"I think we'll have to work on it, Vonnie." I gave her a smile and a kiss on the cheek.

"Cappy, what's got your attention?" I said as it was obvious to me that he was distracted even though he was looking at me.

"One of those at the table with striped shirt, the big one who seems to be their leader has a full color tattoo of an eagle's eye on his neck. It's very unusual," said Cappy. "And, meaningful."

"How is it meaningful?" I said.

"I don't know yet, but it is."

Sometimes Cappy infuriated me.

His cellphone rang, he picked it out of his pocket, answered, said nothing and hung up.

The food arrived and we dug in. Yvonne was quite vocal when eating. She kept making guttural sounds of enjoyment. Cappy and I just ate.

The quintet finished before we did. They got up and left, each of them giving us a glance as they departed.

We ordered coffee and as we waited, Cappy passed around his cell phone. He had a close up of the eagle's eye tattoo.

I said, "how did you get that picture, Cappy?"

"I can make my phone ring when I want it to, so I did and when I picked it up, I snapped a picture of the tattoo. Did I do something wrong?"

"No, Cappy but you sure scare me sometimes."

"Me too," said Yvonne with a frown on her face.

I was aware of the night sounds of the crickets, water lapping on the shore and clinks and clanks of glassware and plates being picked up as I said, "We have a decision to make. Do we move from Red Hook to this marina?"

"What are the risks, Boots?" said Cappy.

"I don't know, Cappy, but it seems to me that we are at risk at the marina in Red Hook. The risk seems like a toss-up. I think we will be closer to an answer if we move here and watch what goes on. Am I making sense?"

"Yes, but I don't like it at all," said Cappy, "however I think you are right that we should move here."

"I don't like it, too," said Yvonne.

"Then it's settled, tomorrow we will sail over here."

"Meanwhile, how did you like your food?" I said.

"Yummy," said Yvonne.

"I agree," said Cappy, "surprisingly good."

"I'm with you too. Yummy and surprisingly good. Denis?"

Denis brought the bill which I paid and left a hefty tip because the service was as good as the food. We walked back to the parking area where to our surprise Gwyneth was waiting, cab door open, to take us back to Red Hook.

"Good evening, you three." Did you enjoy your dinner?

"Good evening Gwyneth, we did," we chimed almost simultaneously as we climbed in for the ten minute ride back to the marina.

We arrived exhausted from the long day and I paid and tipped Gwyneth. We walked to the *Lost & Found* and went in through the aft door. Cappy said he was tired and said, "slaap lekker you two," wishing us a delicious sleep using one of the new Dutch phrases he had learned from Yvonne and went below to his cabin.

Yvonne and I went forward to our cabin and prepared for bed. Lying in bed with the lights out, Yvonne said, "Boots, I am afraid, very afraid."

"Worry not, dear Vonnie. You are safe and have nothing to worry about." I learned over and gave her a kiss.

"I don't hope so," said Vonnie in a soft voice.

I whispered to myself, "I hope not too, Vonnie."

Chapter Twenty-Seven

"Boots?"

"Huh?" I opened my eyes and Yvonne's eyes were just inches away. I could see the flecks of her pupils. "You smell good. Very good." I smiled pulled her lips to mine.

She kissed me and said, "Not now, silly man. Later when we have lots of time, ja? Now we need to get up and move our boat."

"Ok, ok, not now. Later it will be. I'll get up, shower and join you in the salon. But first, I've been saving this to sing to you.
So, "I'm saving my money, to buy you a rainbow, a rainbow, to put on your finger and after I've gone and bought you a rainbow, I'll go out…"

"Yes, you'll go out and what?"

"That's a surprise that I'll sing that for you later."

"That's not fair, Boots."

"Isn't it ok for me to give you a surprise?"

"Well, okey dokies," said Yvonne with a wink. "I love it when you sing to me." She blew me a kiss and left.

I showered, put on my cutoffs with a Club Med Les Almadies T-shirt that I had gotten when I was in Senegal and went into the salon.

Cappy and Yvonne were sitting at the table having coffee. I could hear the murmur voices coming from other boats and people on the docks. We were rocking gently from the wind and waves of passing boats.

"Good morning, Boots," said Cappy, handing me a cup of coffee as I sat down next to Yvonne.

Good morning, you two."

"We made a list, Boots," said Cappy.

"List?"

"Yes, a list of things we need to do today," said Yvonne.

"Ok, I'm all ears."

"Your ears are not so big, lieve Boots."

"He means he is listening with both ears, Yvonne," said Cappy who then read the list. "Buy food at the Marina Market, Fill gas and water tanks. Check out at the marina office. Disconnect electric and water lines. Sail to Cowpet bay, Anchor in the middle somewhere. Yvonne said, she'd buy the food. I'll fill gas and water tanks. Will you check us out of here?"

"I am impressed with your thoroughness. Thank you both and yes, I'll go to the harbormaster and check us out. After I finish my coffee, ok?"

"Okie dokies," said Yvonne.

"What she said," said Cappy with a big grin.

I finished my coffee left the boat. I could feel the sun on my forehead and shoulders as I walked down the dock to the harbormaster's office. I went in and said good morning to the uniformed clerk. There were a few others in casual clothes looking at the magazines and brochures from local businesses that were in a rack off to the side. "I'm in slip 302, the *Lost & Found*. We are moving on so I'd like to pay my bill."

"One moment sir," he said and typed on his computer. "That will be $209.50 including tax."

I handed him my VISA card and said, "Thanks, and if anyone asks, we'll be heading to Saint Croix." I made sure I said it loud enough for everyone in the office to hear.

He handed me back my card and said, "Safe sailing, sir."

I said, "thanks" and left. I could not tell if anyone paid attention to me but I had a hunch I needed to be very careful.

I walked back to my boat and went aboard. Cappy was sitting on the deck, feet up, eyes closed,

"Hey Boots."

"How did you know it was me?"

"I know your walking rhythm and besides, I don't smell any cologne."

"Smartass. Any problems?"

"Nope, not a one. We are all gassed and watered up, Skipper. Yvonne is still at the market. And the cats are napping after spending the morning eyeing a seagull that decided to just sit back here with me."

"Cappy, your safety zone that attracts wild life amazes me. I need to call Red so excuse me a moment, ok?"

"Of course, Cap'n."

"Which is it, Cap'n or Skipper?" I said as I speed-dialed Red.

"Tis which ever word comes to mind at the time, Skippy," said Cappy.

I gave him the finger.

Chapter Twenty-Eight

"Red, Boots here. Can you talk?"

"Sure, Boots, what's up?"

"I want to put you on speaker phone so Cappy can listen, ok with you?"

"Sure. Hi, Cappy."

"Hi, Red. Good to hear your voice."

"Red, we need you here on St. Thomas. Not only has your agent been killed, I am pretty sure we are being followed and that it has to do with the murders he was investigating."

"Why do you think you are being followed?"

"Red, Cappy here. The same guy followed Yvonne and me when we went for a walk. He has been at the same restaurant we've eaten at twice and he has the look of being up to no good.. Also one of his friends has a color tattoo of an eagle's eye on his neck."

"Whoa, Cappy. Are you sure about the eagle's eye tat?"

"Yes, I'm sure, Red, why?"

"I've seen something in one of our BOLOs about that."

"BOLO?"

"Be on the lookout for. I'll look in the computer. Meanwhile, how soon do you need me there?"
"I think we need you yesterday, Red," I said.

"Ok, you two, sit tight. I'll get on the afternoon American flight from Miami. It connects through San Juan and arrives in St. Thomas at 3pm. Where will I meet you?"

"Ask the driver to take you to Bonnie's by the Sea restaurant in Cowpet Bay. Well meet you there at 5, ok?"

"Ok, see you then."

"Travel Gently, Red," said Cappy.

"Hi, gentlemens," said Yvonne, standing on the dock. "Help me with these foods, please." She pointed at a cart full of brown market bags.

"Looks like you bought enough for an army for a month, Vonnie," I said.

"The way you two eat, I think maybe I don't have enough."

"No comment," said Cappy.

We brought the packages up and stowed them.

"What's the plan, Boots?" asked Cappy.

"We will motor out of here, then sail east north east, about 1.5 miles, until we are abeam of Grass Cay, then about 1.2 miles southwest until we are abeam of Great St. James Christmas Cover, then northwest into Cowpet Bay, about a half a mile. We'll use the GPS to know when to change course. Any questions?"

"No," said, Yvonne. "Yes, Boots," said Cappy, "What do we do when we get to Cowpet Bay?"

"When we get into Cowpet Bay, we anchor in the middle of the other boats."

"You two ready?"

"Yes, dear." "Aye, aye, Cap'n"

"Okay then. Cap, forward to the bow line, Yvonne, aft to yours."

I started the engine. "Boots and Yvonne, undo your lines." I put it into gear and carefully pulled away from the dock. We had tied up facing northeast, pointing out of Vessup Bay so only a slight course correction was necessary. I kept us at a moderate speed, and watched the GPS for our turning point.

Yvonne and Cappy came to the cockpit and stood with me, facing the cooling breeze. The sun was strong and we quickly shed our shirts. Yvonne's skimpy halter was a distraction so I started to think about pink elephants. It didn't help very much at all.

We were followed by a few seagulls, circling our wake, screeching, looking for food scraps. The GPS beeped so I turned us southwest to a heading of 225°. The birds followed.

Cappy and Yvonne went aft a few feet and sat behind me on the deck sofa, engrossed in conversation. The GPS beeped again and I turned us northwest into Cowpet Bay.

I slowed us down to just a crawl. "Yo. Cappy and Vonnie. We need to anchor in between some of the boats in the bay. Anything stand out in the middle?"

They looked around as I moved forward, just fast enough to make way. "How about between the motorsailer, 'Delight' and that big Wheeler, 'Done that', Boots?" asked Cappy.
"Ok Cap, go forward and get the bow anchor ready, Vonnie, get the stern anchor ready."

"Aye, skipper," came their shouts

"Throw it Cap," I shouted.

I heard the splash and I put us in reverse and very slowly backed up.

"Ok," yelled Cap. I put us in forward gear for a count of 5 and then to neutral.

"Vonnie, drop yours" I said over my shoulder. As soon as I heard the kerplop, I put us in forward gear.

"She's tightening up, Boots," shouted Yvonne. I put us in neutral and turned off the engine.

"Ok, let's talk. Vonnie, would you get us some wine? Cappy some glasses? I will put up the cover so we can have some shade."

As I put up the cover, I did some figuring. We were about a tenth of a mile from the St. Thomas yacht club beach and just slightly further from the beach at Bonnie's in the middle of about three dozen boats of different types and sizes. Hiding in plain sight as Cappy had said earlier.

"I have a bottle of 'Pouilly Fumé de la Ducette', Boots," said Yvonne. "And I brought up some cheese and crackers.

"I have glasses, Boots," said Cappy

"If I had to choose, I'd take the bottle and not the glasses. And, for the record, that is superb wine, Yvonne." I got a whiff of some broiling meat but the wine and cheese would hold me until dinner.

Yvonne put the cheese and crackers on the table and poured us some wine. I took a cracker, spread some cheese on it, munched a bit, then took my glass and had a sip of my wine.

"Thanks for the wine, cheese and crackers. Thanks for the good company too. I have a question. Cappy and Vonnie, can you two keep tabs on the comings and goings between the boats in here and the shore? Without it being obvious?"

They looked at each other for a moment. Cappy said, "Aye Aye, Skippy." Yvonne smiled and gave me a smart salute.

"I'm going to get our zodiac in the water and make sure there is fuel on board. You two keep your eyes open."

I went aft and swung the davit out past the stern platform, then lowered the zodiac into the water. I checked the gas can to make sure it was full and lowered it on a rope to the platform. I climbed down onto the platform, untied the gas can and lowered myself into the zodiac. I reached up for the gas can and put it in the stern of the zodiac after which I connected the gas can hose to the engine hose. I climbed up to the platform and then up to the deck where I found Cappy and Yvonne looking through binoculars.

"You two see anything?"

"Well, yes, I was just writing it down when you came back on deck, Boots," said, Cappy.

"I'm watching to see what happens next," said, Yvonne.

"What is going on?" I said.

"We both noticed a zodiac come from seemingly nowhere to go to the beach by Bonnie's and a man waded out and got on. We think it's striped shirt but they are so distant it's hard to tell," said, Cappy. "Yvonne's following them with her binocs."

"Look there, Boots," said Yvonne, pointing towards the northeast.

I could just barely make out a zodiac not going fast enough to get attention. "Where the devil is he going? There's nothing there but empty cove.

"Wait, he just disappeared," said, Yvonne.

The three of us stared into the cove, baffled.

"You know, I think I need to take the zodiac out for a test run, just to make sure she's ok for us to use."

"Good idea, Cap'n," said Cappy

"I don't think so too, but be careful, Boots," said Yvonne.

Chapter Twenty-Nine

"I want you two to just sit and play backgammon or sit and read. In other words, relax and do not act like you are paying attention to anything happening in the bay."

"Okey dokies" said Yvonne.

I went over the transom with my cell phone in the pocket of my cut-offs and sat down in the rear of the zodiac.

The engine started easily. I set the throttle to about half and steered southeast for about .2 mile until I was in the shipping channel between Cowpet Bay and St. James Bay. I then turned southwest for about .4 mile and turned northwest, totally out of sight of anyone in Cowpet Bay who might be watching.

I did all this in the hopes that I would look like someone who had some business on the Nazareth area of the island rather than someone on a spying mission.

I trolled around a bit until a half hour had passed and then reversed course. As I neared the entrance to Cowpet Bay, I took my cell phone out and called Yvonne.

She picked up, "Boots, is anything wrong? Why are you calling?"

"Vonnie, listen carefully. I want you to keep the phone up to your ear and talk to me, even if I don't respond. I want to try to take some pictures with my phone but not look like I am, okay?"

"Yes, dear, I get it."

I kept the phone to my ear but pointed at a slight angle so it would be aimed into the cove on the north side of Cowpet Bay. I started the camera recording video on wide focus. I went a bit faster because I only had about 10 minutes of video recording time. As I turned northeast, I let the phone be parallel to my head, still pointing at the cove. I hope I was convincing to anyone watching. I was not convinced.

"Vonnie, I'm approaching you now so we can hang up. Blow me a kiss, please." I hung up and waved. She blew a kiss which I returned. I tied up the zodiac and clambered over the platform and transom.

"So?"

"Cappy I'll tell you both about *so* after we look at the video that I took on the way back. Let's go in the cabin so we can't be seen."

"Would you like some wine?" asked Yvonne.

"I'd love some of that la Doucette if there is any left," I said.

"So would I, Yvonne," said Cappy.

Yvonne poured and I transferred the video from the phone to my laptop.

"Ok, here we go," I said and started the video playback.

After we watched it to the end, I said, "I saw nothing at all. I'm baffled."

"Boots, can you zoom in and play the last two minutes?" asked Cappy

"Sure." I hit the zoom button. "Where are you looking? What am I missing?"

"Do you see the last house on left on the hill above the cove?"

"Yes."

"Look straight down. I see a mast of some sort, maybe a high running light. I see something there."

Yvonne yelped with excitement, "I see it, I see it."

I zoomed in a bit more. "I see it too, Cappy," I said.

"How do you find out what's there?" asked Yvonne.

"That is a very good question," said Cappy

"A KellyHooper?" asked Yvonne.

Cappy and I laughed at the same time.

"A what?" asked Cappy.

"You know. Zeech, it makes noise, whoosh woosh woosh. Hangs in the sky." She spread out he hands and made a spinning motion.

"A helicopter?" I said.

"Yes, that's what I said." said Yvonne with a grin.'

"It's a good idea but I think it's too obvious. I think I need to take a sight-seeing walk this evening."

"Boots, what are you thinking?"

"Cappy, you know that night vision scope you have?"

"Yes?"

"I need to borrow it this evening."

"Uh oh," said, Yvonne.

"Yeah, uh oh." said, Cappy

"I'll explain over dinner with Red. It's almost time to get going, so do what you need to do to get ready. How about we leave at 4:30? And, Cappy, bring the scope."

 "Ok but I do not like this at all," said Cappy.

"I don't too." said, Yvonne.

I gave her a hug and whispered, "I love you."

Cappy smiled and said, "What else is new?"

Chapter Thirty

A small storm cloud rushed by, fierce but fast, the rain almost dry before it hit the ground. When the lightning ended, we lowered ourselves into the zodiac and started across the bay just before 4:30. I kept the throttle at a very slow speed.

"What is that? Wow, what is that?" asked Yvonne looking into the water on her left.

I saw the shape under the water, moving very slowly, almost as big as the zodiac. "Yvonne, that is a sea turtle, they hang around here but I don't know why."

"Are they dangerous?"

"Cappy?" I deferred to him when it came to the habits of nature's creatures.

"I doubt it but I do not know for sure," replied Cappy.

As we approached Bonnie's, I said, "Cappy would you hop off the zodiac onto that small dock and tie us up?"

"Aye aye, Cap'n."

"Would you stop calling me Cap'n?"

"Sure thing, Skipper."

"That too."

He smiled and stepped onto the dock. Yvonne followed.

I got off the zodiac saw Denis who waived.

"Good evening, Mr. Boots. How are you?"

"Very well, Denis, and you?"

"I'm well, sir. Would you like a table for three?"

"Four, please. We are expecting someone else."

He led me to a table by the water where I was quickly joined by Cappy and Yvonne.

"Cappy, why do you insist on calling me Cap'n or Skippy, etc?"

"Why not?"

I asked myself how I could argue with him when he responds that way and I had no answer.

"How about a drink while waiting for Red?"

"Rum Punch for me, Boots."

"Singapore Fling for me," said, Yvonne.

"It's a Singapore Sling, Vonnie. A fling is something else entirely." I motioned to Denis who came over and took our drink order.

"What's a fling?" asked Yvonne.

"Yeah, Ca.. I mean Boots, what's a fling?"

"Well, to describe one I'd have to…" Just then I saw Red getting out of a taxi in the parking lot. "Here comes Red."

Red saw us and walked to our table. He went straight to Yvonne and gave her a hug. "Hey gorgeous, long time no see. Cappy and Boots, have a seat, I'm not hugging you too."

We all sat, Denis appeared with our drinks and addressed Red, "Sir, would you like a drink?"

"A Rum Punch, please."

"I like this Singapore thing," said Yvonne.

"I'm glad, Vonnie," I said, giving her hand a squeeze.

"Red, did you ever find out what info Carl knew that he never got to tell me before he was killed?"

"No, we never did, Boots. He had nothing in his notes except the word 'birds' with a bunch of question marks."

"Good grief." said Cappy.

"Here you are, sir," said Denis and put Reds drink on the table.

"What, Cappy?" asked Red.

"I said, Good Grief. Look at it, 'birds', and an 'eagle eye' tattoo on someone's neck? Bingo." said Cappy.

"Yes, but what does it mean?" I said.

"That is for us to figure out," said Red, "but it can't be a coincidence. And, Carl was one smart agent."

We sat and sipped our drinks. The tree frogs were chirring, a few iguanas scurried about, clinks and clanks reached our ears from the kitchen and we heard murmurings from neighboring tables.

"Are you ready to order, lady and gentlemen?" asked Denis.

We had not discussed ordering at all. I asked the table, "How about we let Denis decide what to order for us?" Yvonne smiled and winked while Cappy and Red nodded their assent. "Dennis, it's up to you."

"Yes sir. I promise you will be pleased."

"Do not look now, but here comes striped shirt," said Cappy softly.

From the Eagle Chronicles # 9

"I'm pulling alongside now, Eagle," said, Buzz

"I see you, Buzz," said Eagle.

Buzz handled the sub easily, rising just above the surface. Tayana with Falcon at the helm was on her starboard side. She saw Falcon step off *Tayana* and felt his weight on the sub as he walked over to *Raptor.*

Buzz turned off the engine and the power to the system.

She opened the hatch, enjoying the splashes of water, a relief from the cramped quarters of the sub. She hoisted herself quickly through the hatch, closing it and pushing the button that would automatically lower the sub out of sight.

"Hey Eagle and Falcon," she said as she climbed on board *Raptor.*

"Hey yourself, Buzz. Grab a beer and join us," said Eagle.

"I need to use the loo, guys. Be right back," said, Buzz.

Buzz went below and thought, *"How am I going to get away from these two fucking lunatics? How?"*

Chapter Thirty-One

"Well, take a gander at his entourage." said Red, "Three men and a woman are with him."

"That's the same group as before, Red," I said.

"Gander? Like a man goose?" asked Yvonne quizzically.

"It's an expression meaning to take a look, Vonnie," said Cappy.

"You Americans. Such words you use. Hah."

"And this time I see something I didn't see before," said Cappy quietly.

"What?" I said.

"They all have a tattoo of the eye of a raptor on their neck. They are too far away for me to be specific," responded Cappy

"What's a raptor?" asked Yvonne.

"A bird of prey. A bird that hunts small animals for his food," I said.

"Something about them is very scary," said Yvonne.

"I agree," said Red, "and I'm glad we are talking softly. Very glad. All my alarm bells are going off."

"Mine too," I said.

"Me three," said Yvonne.

"Me four five and six," said Cappy.

Just then Denis arrived with another waiter bringing our food.

There was an assortment of Caribbean delicacies for appetizers and for our entrée, broiled sea bass with a salsa of tomato and crisp baby bok toy tossed with garlic and fresh basil served on a bed of mushroom risotto.

We were quiet as we ate our meal, aside from an occasional "mmm" from one or the other of us.

When we were having Espresso and Sambucca, I said, "While we were eating I happened to glance up and see the tattooed quintet leaving, with striped shirt looking at us over his shoulder. It was not a friendly look."

"Red, could you arrange a sightseeing ride for me?"

"What?"

"I want a tour of the area on the northern hillside overlooking Cowpet Bay. I looked on Google Earth and have a good idea of the layout of the roads above this area."

"When do you want to do this?"

"As soon as Cappy gets hands me his night vision scope."

"Ok," said Red and picked up his cell phone and made a call.

"My car is at your command, Boots."

I felt Cappy hand me a very small package under the table. I gave a slight nod as I took it and put it into the side pocket of my pants.

"His car understands English?" said Yvonne with a puzzled look.

I took her hand, "No, Vonnie, it's one of our English expressions. It means that his driver will do what I ask him to do."

"You Americans are very strange. Very." said Yvonne and gave me a kiss on the cheek.

"Yvonne, Cappy, Listen carefully. Red, let's go into the men's room and switch shirts. I want to create some confusion in case we are being watched. Be right back, ladies."

We got up and went past the bar into the men's room. "Red, when we go out, I'm going to go to the table and say good night. You sit next to Yvonne and enjoy the local music. I'll be back in less than an hour if all goes well. For any onlookers, you are now me."

"Got it. Wait a minute while I call my driver and let him know what's going on." Red picked up his cell phone and did just that.

"Good luck, Boots, and please be careful. Let's go to the table."

Chapter Thirty-Two

We went out of the men's room. I walked as casually as I could to our table. "Boots. Cappy and Yvonne, I've got to go back to the field office for about an hour. Hold the fort."

As I turned I heard Yvonne ask, "Hold a fort? What's a fort?" I smiled as I walked to the parking lot and got into the waiting FBI rent-a-car. The driver turned and said, "Hi, Boots. Red called me from the men's room. My name is Jayden but call me Jay. Where do you want to go?"

"Hi, Jay. Let's go out of the Elysian parking lot and turn right on Cowpet Bay East Estate road keep going for about one quarter of a mile. Then the road will turn south. Another two hundred feet there is a small driveway to the right. Take it to the end."

"Okay, Mr. Boots," said Jay as he started the car and drove slowly up the hill from Bonnie's, past the Elysian hotel offices and toward the exit. The air-conditioning cooled the car quickly and by the time we turned to the east out of the parking lot, the temperature was comfortable.

"Call me Boots, okay?"

"Okay but it's difficult for me. I was raised to say Mr."

"If you call me Mr. Boots, I'll have to call you Mr. Jay. I'd rather we keep it informal."

"I'll try, Mr. er, I mean Boots."

In only a few minutes, we turned south. "Jay, go slow here. According to the maps the driveway is small, unpaved and to our right.

"Here it is, Boots," said Jay as he slowed and turned onto a very narrow dirt road.

"Keep going, Jay."

"This seems to be the end, Boots," said Jay as he stopped the car.

"I should only be a few minutes, Jay. If I am not back in fifteen, please call out the troops." I got out of the car and let my eyes adjust to the fading light of dusk.

I had mental picture of the road from Google Earth and walked slowly on uneven ground towards through the trees. I knew I only had to go about 50 feet. I also knew that there was an abrupt end to this wooded area that ended in sharp drop off to the bay below. I tripped on a tree root and fell, my left knee coming down on a rock, my right elbow breaking my fall. I wound up on all fours, looking like a runner ready to start a sprint. I looked ahead and realized that I was the edge of the cliff was only a few feet in front of me. I took the night-scope out of my pocket, put the loop around my wrist and flattened out on the sand, rocks and tree roots. I looked through the lens, moved around the cove, zoomed, focused and put my finger on the shutter release. I was about to take some pictures when my brain exploded with a blinding pain.

Chapter Thirty-Three

Through a fog I heard, "Boots? Boots, are you ok?"

I opened my eyes slowly because even in the near dark, the slight light hurt. My head hurt a lot worse. "Jay?"

"Yes, its' me, Jay. Are you all right?"

"I don't know yet. What happened?" I stayed on the ground trying to get used to the pain.

"I was sitting in the car with the lights out when I saw a slight reflection of light and then movement about 20 yards away, going in the direction you had gone. I pulled my gun and followed. I saw you lying on the ground with someone standing over you. He must have heard me because he took off like a shot out of hell, back towards the road."

I sat up slowly as the pain lessened. "Did you get a look at him?"

"Not exactly."

"What do you mean, Jay?"

"All I saw was the side of a neck with what looked like an eye on it. It was very bizarre."

"Maybe not so bizarre. Give me a hand?" I extended my arm and he grabbed my hand and helped me stand.

"Whoa."

"Are you ok, Boots?"

"I think so, just dizzy for a moment."

"Boots, I hate to say it but I had an impression of being followed up here, yet there were no lights behind us."

"Well, as far as I'm concerned you saved my life, Jay."

"Let's get back to Bonnies."

"I know a back way, Boots, just in case."

"Fine by me."

We walked to the car and got in. Jay drove only a few minutes before turning sharply to the left onto Tracy Way.

"Where are we, Jay?"

"We are at the condos on the hill above Bonnie's. There is a long flight of stairs going down to the beach."

"I can't just show up down there. I'm supposed to have left for the evening as Red."

"The stairs end up by the men's room. I'm going to call Red on his cell and tell him to go in there and meet you. You two switch shirts. He comes up the stairs, you go out to be with your friends. Okay?"

"Sounds good to me, Jay and thanks."

I got out of the car and went down the stairs. Each step caused a touch of pain in the back of my head. I went into the men's room without having to go through the restaurant.

"Boots, are you ok? You look like hell," said Red as he took off his shirt.

"I'm ok enough, Red. Thank God Jay was alert. He saved my life." I took off my shirt and we switched.

"What did you see up there? I'm dying to know."

"I saw a lot but, please don't use the word, dying. " I said with a smile. "How about I tell you for breakfast? I think if I stay in here any longer it's going to look suspicious. Eight work?" I said as I finished buttoning up.

"Eight it is, my friend," he said, gave me a hug. and left the men's room.

I strolled out as casually as I could and went to the table and sat down.

"So, did you pay the tab while I was in the men's room?" I said, very slightly shaking my head no.

"Are you trying to get away without paying *again*?" asked Cappy.

"Well, heck, I tried," and smiled.

I caught Denis' eye. "Denis, could I have the check please?"

Denis seemed amused by our banter and brought the check, handing it to Cappy with a big grin, then taking it back and handing it to me, saying, "Ooops."

We all laughed. I paid the tab including a nice extra tip for Denis and got up. "Shall we?" I said and pulled Yvonne's chair out for her as she started to rise.

We walked to the dock and got into the zodiac.

I started the engine. "Cappy would you untie us?"

"Yes, Skip.. I mean Boots," he said with a salute.

I took us back to the *Lost & Found,* tied us up to the stern where we climbed onto the afterdeck and went into the lounge.

"Boots are you ok?" asked Yvonne, reaching for my hand, "It looks like the back of your head was bleeding."

"I saw it too but didn't want to ask while we were at Bonnie's," said Cappy.

"I got whacked on the back of the head while I was looking through your night scope, Cappy. Red's driver saw movement and came to look for me. He saved my life."

"Oh, lieve Boots," said Yvonne giving me a hug. "Let me clean that wound." She went to get the first aid kit.

"What did you see, Boots," asked Cappy.

"A lot. I'll tell you when Yvonne gets back," I said, rubbing the back of my head. I took his night scope out of my pocket and handed it to him.

"Hey, there is a new picture in here. You must have snapped it when you got hit."

I heard Yvonne come up behind me. "Easy, Vonnie, it's tender," I said as I felt her fingers on my scalp.

"Oh, you big baby. I'm sorry but I need to get the dirt out of the wound."

"Gee, thanks."

"Goed voor jou, goed voor niets." said Yvonne with a smile.

"What did she say, Boots?"

She said, "Good for you, good for nothing. With her it's a term of endearment."

"Heaven help us," said Cappy. "Look at this picture you took."

While Yvonne had been cleaning my wound, Cappy had plugged the camera's memory card into my laptop.

"I see four people, looks like four of the one's from the restaurant at dinner, sitting on the fantail of a yacht. They have glasses in their hands and it looks like they are having a toast. Who is missing?" I said.

"Striped shirt isn't there and I'd bet he is the one who whacked you. Where did you see the yacht, Boots?"

"Remember when we thought we saw the top of a mast in the cove?"

"Yes, I do, but.."

"Wait. Cappy there is an outcropping of rock. It rises a dozen or more feet above the water. Behind that outcropping is a yacht. I think it's a motorsailer, perhaps 60 to 70 feet in length. Here's the kicker.."

"Kicker?" asked Yvonne.

"It means the surprise, Vonnie."

"What's the surprise?"

"Behind the yacht, between the yacht and the rocks, hidden from view except from where, by chance I was looking, was a small sailboat and between the sailboat and the yacht was what seemed to be a small submarine. "

"It doesn't show in the picture, Boots," said Cappy.

"I'm not surprised since I was trying to zoom in on the after deck to catch their faces, but it was there."

"That would explain a lot, Boots."

"What do you mean, Cappy," asked Yvonne.

"Having a small sub would explain how people were surprised and captured without time to send an SOS," he responded. "And as to the small sailboat, I'm not sure but I don't like it at all, at all."

"Thanks Cappy. We'll talk more about it. Meanwhile you two, I'm exhausted. Totally and we need to get early so I can meet Red at eight."

"You mean *you* need to get up early. I am going to sleep in," said, Cappy."

"I am coming to bed with you, Boots," said Yvonne who then gave Cappy a hug. "Good night, Cappy, "Slaap lekker."

"Come, lieve Boots," said Yvonne, pulling me gently toward our cabin. "Shh, don't talk, I know you are hurting and tired. Lie down, slaap lekker, lieve Boots, slaap lekker."

I went out like a light. And I did slaap lekker with her beside me.

Chapter Thirty-Four

I woke up at the crack of dawn, Yvonne's hair on my cheek, her eyes looking into my eyes as they opened. "Your eyes are like the eyes of a cat, Boots. I love them."

"What a wonderful way to wake up. Thank you, lieve Vonnie."

"You have to meet Red in an hour. Do we have time for a shower? Maybe together to save water?"

"We must save water, Vonnie. That is surely necessary."

After our shower, we went into the lounge.

"No sign of Cappy so let's take our coffee out on deck," I suggested.

"Ja, let's."

I settled onto one of the fantail cushions and said, "Vonnie, I want you and Cappy to stay on board until I return. Do not leave under any circumstances, okay?"

"Are you worried?"

"I am just being cautions, Vonnie."

"Ok, I'll tell Cappy. We can spend time people eyeing. We both love to do it."

"Good idea. Time for me to go. I should be back by noon. If not, I'll call you on your cell."

We both stood up and I pulled her to me for a hug and long kiss.

"I love you, Boots."

"I love you too, Vonnie. I'll see you later."

I went aft, stepped down into the zodiac, started the engine, undid the bow line and cast off. Yvonne blew me a kiss as I waved and turned away from the boat and headed for shore.

A smiling hostess greeted me, "Good morning, Sir. Table for one?"

I read her name tag. "Good morning, Isabel. I'll be joined by another gentlemen. We'd like to sit over there by the water's edge."

"Very good, sir. Right this way please."

I sat facing the *Lost & Found* and could see Yvonne sitting on the afterdeck looking towards me. There was a gentle breeze coming across the bay. I waved and as she waved back I saw Red sit down in the chair next to me. He waved at Yvonne and said, "Good morning, Boots, how are you feeling today?"

"My head is a tad sore but aside from that, I'm worried."

"Why?"

"Gentlemen? Would you like to order?" asked Isabel as she came to the table from behind me.

"Coffee and a Danish for me, please, Isabel. Red?"

"Same here, please."

"Coming right up, sirs."

"I worry that someone, seemingly striped shirt followed me, thinking it was you. I wonder why. I'm worried that they will put a hit on you as they did with your local agent."

"Yeah, Boots. It's puzzling to say the least. Meanwhile, what did you see last night before you got wacked on the noggin?"

"Here you are, sirs," said Isabel, putting our coffee and Danishes on the table.

I told Red what I told Yvonne and Cappy the evening before and he said, "Submarine? Good grief, the implications are staggering, Boots. We have literally dozens and dozens of unsolved disappearances in the Caribbean each year and this could explain some of them. What are your plans?"

"I was hoping the FBI would step in, Red."

"We don't have any evidence tying them to anything at all. Nothing to warrant a search warrant, that's for sure."

"Well, what about the sub?"

"It's not illegal to own one, Boots."

"What about askin…"

"I've got an idea if the locals would go along with it. Hmm."

"What, Red?"

"I think it would be logical to check all the boats in Cowpet Bay for their registrations as part of a routine spot check looking for drugs. We'd start with the boats closest to Bonnie's and fan out to the cove where that yacht and sub are."

"Great idea. When can you get it in motion?"

"It'll take the rest of the day to set it up, so I'd think tomorrow morning we can start the inspections.. And I'll have a Coast Guard cruiser stationed in the entrance to Cowpet bay just in case."

"Terrific."

"I'll be one of the inspectors and we'll inspect your boat as well."

"Okey dokey. See you in the morning, Red. Go do your stuff. I'll settle up."

"See ya, Boots." Red got up and walked to the parking lot and his waiting driver.

I saw Isabel off to the side, wiping a table. "Isabel, may I have the check please?"

"Of course sir. Was everything satisfactory this morning?" She put the bill on the table in front of me.

"Yes, very. Thank you and have a wonderful day." I paid with a handsome tip as well.

"You too, sir," she said with a grin.

I walked to the zodiac, got in, started it up, untied and putted out to the *Lost & Found* and my girl.

Chapter Thirty-Five

I got back to my boat about 9:30. There was a slight chop in the bay as I rode back. I tied up the zodiac and climbed up to the fantail. Cappy was sitting on one of the stern seats feeding bits of his omelet to Pietje and Stafje who were sitting on the table facing him.

"Yo, Boots. Top of the morning to you."

"Top to you too, Cap.." How are the kitties?"

"P & S are fine, so is Yvonne," he said with a wink. "How did it go with Red?"

Yvonne came up behind me and put her arms around my neck, and said, "Yes, this kitty of yours is fine too, lieve."

"Ok, here's the scoop," and I told them about the discussion I had with Red."

"So, we sit and wait?" asked Cappy.

"Yes, indeed. And, in the meanwhile, there are chores to be done on board our trusty home."

"I have an important meeting to attend in Monaco," said Cappy.

"Me too," said, Yvonne.

"As soon as you do the chores, you may leave for Monaco."

"Yeah, yeah, ok, what do we have to do, Skipper?" asked Cappy.

"Make believe you are crew on this boat and raise anchor so we can motor all the way over to the St. Thomas Yacht Club dock about seven hundred feet west of here and fill our gas and water tanks."

"That's an awful lot to ask, Skip," said Cappy as he went forward towards the bow.

"Me too," said Yvonne who stood by the stern anchor line.

"Ready, Cap'n," came the voice from the bow.

"Ready, Cap'n," said Yvonne

"You two. What a pair." I went up to the bridge and started the engines. "Raise anchors, mates."

We wove between the anchored boats to the marina's T-dock and pulled abeam of it.

"I've got the bow line, Boots," said Cappy.

"I've got the stern," said Yvonne.

A young man came out, and said, "Good morning. What can I do for you?"

"Fill us up with gas and top off our water supply as well, if you please," I said.

"Yes, sir."

"Yvonne, would you feed Pietje and Stafje while Cappy and I clean the decks?"

"Aye, aye, Cap'n," she said with her usual grin.

"Cappy, it's your fault."

"What is?"

"That she calls me Cap'n."

"I plead the fifth."

"Ok, Ok, wise guy. Let's hose down the decks."

Out of the blue, Yvonne started to giggle.

I was about to ask her why she was giggling when she said, "Boots, what does pop goes the weasel mean?"

"Huh?" Cappy and I said, almost simultaneously.

"What does pop goes the weasel mean?" she said again with a silly giggle.

"Why are you asking this?"

"Because I want to know, silly."

"I don't know the answer, Vonnie, but what on earth prompted did you to ask?"

She giggled and said, "While you were at breakfast with Red and Cappy was still asleep, I turned on the TV and there was a re-run of something called, NYPD Blue and this cop named Andy something I can't pronounce was in the police car with his partner and asked him what pop goes the weasel means."

"Yes, and?" I said.

She started to giggle again, "His partner said he didn't know."

"So why are you giggling, Vonnie?" asked Cappy.

"Because this cop named Andy kept giggling and it was contangerous and I caught it and I can't stop."

"Yvonne, you are a gem," said Cappy stifling a giggle.

Now I giggled too. "You are right, Vonnie, it is contangerous. Contagious too."

Thank God the marina employee hailed us or we might still be giggling. He had a strange look on his face as he said, "All full with both gas and water, sir. How will you be paying?"

I handed him my credit card which he took and walked to the marina office to run the charge.

"Vonnie, what made you think of that question?" I said.

"Because that marina guy reminds me of a weasel," she said giggling.

Cappy put his hand over his mouth as the marina guy came back with my card and the slip for me to sign.

I signed, took my card and said, "Thanks for the fill ups and have a great day."

"Cappy, Vonnie, to your stations. Let's go back to our anchorage."

Chapter Thirty-Six

We'd had a light lunch on the fantail, and were just relaxing, taking in the sun, listening to the seagulls and the waves and the clinks of the halyards on the mast.

"Red and I made a decision," I said during lunch. "When that Coast Guard cutter inspects us, I am going to get on board. I'll put on my dress up white slacks and shirt and I'll look enough like one of the inspectors to pass for one of them."

"For God's sake, why, Boots?" asked Cappy.

"So I can then slip onto that small sailboat moored alongside the sub and the bigger one. I've got to know what's going on over there."

"You are putting your life on the… ," started Cappy.

"Boots, look," said Yvonne, pointing to the Coast Guard cutter which had just entered Cowpet bay from the East. It was a majestic sight to see, it's red and white and blue vertical striped bow breasting the waves. It was slowing so as to not cause too much bouncing for the boats that were moored in the bay.

"What a beautiful sight," I said. "Now we wait."

"Great," said Cappy throwing his hands up in the air.

"Cappy, didn't' we come here to try to find Bebe and stumble onto something much bigger?"

"Yes, but.."

"And didn't we promise Julie we'd give it our all?"

"Yes, but..."

"And aren't we out in this bay to work with Red to stop whoever is doing this heinous things?"

"Yes, but, oh blast it, ok, ok but be careful, please. There is only one of you and I don't want to lose you."

"Amen," said, Yvonne with a wink.

"Boots, I'm watching the cutter go from boat to boat in the bay. How are you going to manage this?"

"Cappy, I have my white outfit laid out in my cabin. When they board, I'll go below with them, come back up dressed in the whites and get on the cutter with them. The last boat to be inspected will be the one hidden in the north part of the cove."

"What will happen when they realize that you are not here with us, Boots?" asked Yvonne.

"I think they will be too busy watching the Cutter to be thinking about any of us." And to myself I said, *"I sure hope I'm right."*

Just as I heard the deep throated, yet subdued roar of marine engines, Cappy said, "It looks like we're next, Boots."

"When I leave with the cutter, I want you two to go below and lock up. Do not let anyone on this boat. Cappy, you know where the shark rifle is, right?"

"Yes, Boots, but how will we know what's going on?"

"Ja, how?" echoed Yvonne.

"I'll get word to you as soon as I can. I'm taking a waterproof cell phone as well as a gun with me in a waterproof pouch. Red has both of your cell phone numbers as well, so rest easy."

"Yeah, easy for you to say." said Cappy

"Ja." said, Yvonne.

Chapter Thirty-Seven

"Request permission to come aboard," asked one of the Coast Guard crew. They had pulled long side and thrown a line which I grabbed and tied to a stern cleat. Cappy grabbed tied one off at the bow.

"Permission granted," I replied and they came one by one onto the fantail.

"Commander Smythe with seamen Janes, McMurdey, Hylund and Rang, sir. This is a routine inspection. May I see your papers while the rest examine your boat?"

"Of course, Lieutenant. Let's go to the bridge, shall we." One sailor stayed on deck with Yvonne, the rest of us went forward. Cappy stayed with the lieutenant handling the paperwork while I went to my cabin with one of the sailors and did a quick change into my whites while the other two went aft to give a cursory inspection, as per the arrangements made by Red with the local Coast Guard Commander.

"Mr. Beaumont, when we go out on deck, I suggest we do it quickly and get off as fast as we can. You go in the middle of the pack and go below."

"Good thinking, Commander, and while you do that my friends will stay on the bridge and move around as much as possible to avoid a clear count of heads. I'm ready as I'll ever be."

"Ok, let's roll." We went to the bridge, and not surprisingly, the others were all gathered around Yvonne. Cappy looked amused.

I gave Yvonne a quick hug and I walked to the fantail in the middle of the five Coast Guardsmen where we quickly left the *Lost & Found.* We went below decks on the cutter as fast as we could where, even though I was worried, I breathed a sigh of relief to be below. I quickly changed out of my whites. I had worn a bathing suit so I was ready to go.

I heard the engines go into gear as we got underway. I knew we were headed towards the mystery ship and sub.

"Mr. Rang, How do you plan to get me offloaded?"

"We'll be tied up across their stern with our stern facing north towards the sub. When our crew is all on deck of the mystery ship we will ask that all hands be in their lounge for a head count before the inspection. You'll see the after-deck empty. That will be your signal to go over our stern, and hopefully inspect the sub and smaller boat."

"Sounds good."

"Also, Mr. Beaumont, I have two items that the Commander wanted you to take with you." and he handed me two little metallic boxes.

"What are these, Mr. Rang?"

"I thought you knew, sir. These are tracking devices. Remove the tape on the side and place anywhere below water on the side of the sub and the sailboat. The salt in the water will activate and power them for at least a month. We'll be able to track both of them with these. They are brand new and work well."

I took the two trackers and put them in the plastic bag with my cell phone and gun and clipped it to my waist band.

"We'll be going on deck now. Good luck, Mr. Beaumont."

"Thanks for all your help, guys."

I felt us slowing down and heard the boat shift into neutral.

"Ahoy *Raptor*, This is the US Coastguard."

Raptor, I thought, *that sure goes with those tattoos.*

"Yes, Coastguard?"

"Request permission to come aboard for a routine inspection."

"Of course, sir."

I heard the sounds of us tying up to the boat, then the conversation from above.

"Welcome aboard. My name is 'Stephen Gage'.

"Mr. Gage, My name is Commander Smythe. Please have all your hands come into the lounge for a head count."

"Of course, Commander. You heard him. All hands into the lounge."

I parted the curtain and watched through the porthole. I saw that the afterdeck was empty, crossed my fingers and went up the ladder to the stern which was facing away from *Raptor*.

I lowered myself over the transom of the cutter, climbed down the boarding ladder and got into the water. I expected to be near the sub but I didn't see it. Only the sailboat. Where the devil was the sub? I sure couldn't go diving for it. I swam the few feet to the stern of the sailboat which was nestled against the starboard side of *Raptor*. Off to my right I could see a shadow underwater. It had to be the sub. I knew Commander Smythe would prolong the inspection but I didn't know how much time I had before I had to get to the sailboat and back to the cutter. The sub would have to wait… at least I knew where it was.

The name on the rear of the sailboat was "Salt Spring" but as I lifted myself over the stern and into the cockpit, I brushed against the side of the boat and realized that the name was slightly raised from the rest of the surface. I stayed low in the cockpit, unlatched the cabin door and crawled through into the cabin before standing up. It was late in the day so it was fairly dim inside the lounge but I saw a sparkle under the dining table. I crouched down and picked up a gold ankle bracelet. I turned over the heart and saw "Bebe" engraved on its surface. I knew then that this was Tayana and that Bebe and Winston were dead. I put the anklet into my plastic bag. I saw nothing else that would help and I knew I needed to get out and fast.

I took a peek through the hatch and saw no one on the fantail of the yacht so I stayed low as I went into the cockpit, latched the cabin door, went to the stern of the sailboat and lowered myself over the starboard side of the sailboat, away from *Raptor*. It was still quiet and I knew I needed to try to get to the sub. I took one of the trackers out of the bag, took a deep breath and dived. The water was murky but enough light came down to allow me to aim at the sub and reach it. It was about 20 feet below the surface and I could hold my breath for 3 minutes if I had to. I grabbed onto the side of the sub, went as low as I could, removed the tape from the tracker and pressed it against the side of the sub. I went straight up, almost out of breath, but careful not to gasp when I reached the surface. I took the second tracker out of the bag, took off the tape and placed it below the waterline of the sailboat's starboard side.

I was about to swim to the cutter when I heard voices and saw people on the fantail of the *Raptor*. I quickly pulled myself to the port side of the sailboat, hidden from view. *"Shit, now I can't get on the cutter without being seen. How on earth can I get back to my boat?"*

Chapter Thirty-Eight

I was trying to figure out if I could swim back to my boat when I heard voices from the deck of *Raptor*.

"Mr. Danker," asked Smythe in a rather loud and annoyed voice.

"Yes, Commander?"

"That sailboat," he said, pointing to the smaller vessel.

"Yes, Commander… What about it?"

"Do you have papers for it?"

"Of course, Commander, let me get them for you," said Danker who turned and went into the cabin.

Smythe had slowly moved forward, the crew of both boats following him. I knew he did this to give me a chance to get back. I ducked under the water, swam to the stern of the cutter, edged myself around to the port side and climbed up the ladder to the deck of the cutter and on my belly crawled into the cabin and waited. I closed my eyes and pictured Yvonne smiling at me.

I was still seeing her visage when about ten minutes later I heard Smythe say, "Mr. Beaumont, are you okay?"

"Yes, Captain, just relaxing."

"What did you find out?"

"I saw the shadow of the sub abaft of the sailboat. The name of the sailboat was obviously changed. There is a wooden board with a new name over the old one. Inside the sailboat I found an anklet that I know belongs to my friend, Bebe. I fear she and her groom are dead."

"I'm sorry, Mr. Beaumont."

"Thanks, Commander. How can I get back on my own boat?"

"I think we'll go back through the bay slowly and close enough to your boat that you can go overboard on our starboard side and swim to your boat undetected. Is that all right with you?"

"It sure is," I said as I felt the cutter get underway.

"You'll find some plastic evidence bags below, so take one and put your 'whites' into it to keep them dry when you swim over to your boat. We'll be there in a minute or so."

"Thanks, Commander to you and your crew, for all your help."

"Glad to be of service. Good luck with your investigation."

I went below, put my clothes into a plastic bag and went back to the cabin. I felt the cutter slowing and one of the deck hands said, "You should go over the starboard side now, Mr. Beaumont. Your boat is about 100 feet abeam of us. Push off hard so you are well clear our props as we go by. Good luck sir."

I thanked him, climbed down the ladder they had put out for me, plastic bag hanging around my neck, pushed off against the hull of the cutter and started swimming. I could see the lights of *Lost & Found* in front of me in the darkness. I did not like swimming when I could not see what was below me. My experiences with sharks gave me terrifying images as I made my way to my own boat, my haven, Cappy, and my Vonnie.

I swam to the far side, away from the view of *Raptor* in case anyone was looking. I rapped on the hull and called out softly, "Yo, Cappy, Yvonne?" Nothing. I rapped again. I called out a bit louder, "Cappy, Yvonne."

"Where are you," asked Yvonne. We hear you but can't see you."

"Starboard side, near the stern. No flashlight, just come over and give me a hand."

Chapter Thirty-Nine

"Hi, Cappy," I said as I took the hand I saw extended over the side of my boat. I pulled myself up to the walk-around and went into the cabin.

"How did you know it was me instead of Yvonne?" asked Cappy?

"Yvonne does not have hairy hands, that's how."

Yvonne giggled. "I always knew you were all wet, lieve Boots," said Yvonne as she gave me a towel.

"Danke." I went below to my cabin, stripped off the soggy bathing suit, dried off and put on a pair of ragged cut-offs an old T-shirt. I took my 'whites' out of the plastic bag and hung them in my clothes locker. I took my cell phone out of the plastic bag and put it in my pocket. I threw the bag in the trash and went back to the cabin.

"Are you two okay?" I said.

"Yes," said Cappy, "we are. What happened out there?"

"Well… " I told them what I had done with the tracking devices.

"Yes, and?" said, Cappy.

"And?"

"Boots, I know you are holding back. What else went on?"

"I…" Unexpected tears flooded my eyes, a very unusual thing for me to have happen.

Yvonne put her hand over mine and said, "What, lieve Boots?"

"I found Bebe's anklet on the deck of the sailboat. Its name had been changed but it's no doubt the one they rented. I've no doubt they were killed." Yvonne tightened her grip on my hand and whispered "I'm sorry," in my ear.

"I'm sorry Boots, truly sorry," said Cappy, would you like me to call Julie and let her know?"

"Actually, yes Cappy, I'd like that. I don't know how to do it the way you can."

"Be right back," said Cappy as he headed for his bunkroom, his cell phone already in his hand.

"Vonnie, I need to speak to Red," I said as I gave her a hug.

I took my cell phone out and dialed.

He didn't waste time. "Boots, Hi, I heard what happened from Commander Smythe. I'm so sorry. Is there anything I can do?"

"Yes there is. We need to talk. "

"We need a place where we'll not be seen together, Boots."

"I have an idea, Red. There is an Elysian Beach condo sales office next to Bonnie's. There is a back door that you can get to from the upper roadway that goes to the Ritz-Carlton. Can you get there without being followed?"

"You bet I can. When?"

"Well, the sign on the rental office says it opens at 9am. Can you make it?"

"How about 9:30, Boots?"

"Ok. See you in the morning."

I saw that Cappy had come back to the lounge. "Are you okay, Cappy?"

"Okay enough but telling someone a relative dies sucks. And when it's someone you care about, it's ten times worse. Through her tears, Julie said to thank you." He wiped the tears from his eyes.

Yvonne went to Cappy and gave him a hug, then turned to me and said, "What are you and Red going to do?"

"Boots?"

 "Yes, Vonnie?"

"Can I change the subject?"

"Sure."

"While you were out, Cappy told me about how you helped that adopted person Todd find his mom. I have a beautiful flight attendant friend named Jung Kyung Sook who was adopted from Korea, taken immediately to Norway and raised in a Caucasian family. She wants to find her first mom and she is in o much pain. We flew together often became friendly and I adore her. Can you help her?"

"God, What a tragedy. It's hard for me to imagine what it's like to not only lose a family but one's motherland as well. I hate that it happens. Sure. Get all the information you can from her and I'll try to help her when we wrap this mystery up, ok?"

"Thanks, Lieve, I'll let her know."

"Ahem. Cappy, since when is it ok to talk about my past cases?"

"Since now. This is different and you can help, right?"

"Yeah, yeah, why is it you are right most of the time?"

"It's because I'm a shrink and I know everything."

"Were."

"Were what?"

"A shrink, you retired."

"Once a shrink, always a shrink."

"Good grief. Vonnie, do you see what I mean?"

"I don't hope so."

"I don't hope so too," said Cappy

"Oh my God, how about we get some sleep? I've got to get up early, to meet Red."

Cappy came and gave Yvonne and me hugs then headed forward to the stairs down to his bunkroom.

Yvonne took my hand, winked and led me to the stairs down to our stateroom saying, "Shhh, lieve, Shhhh."

From the Eagle Chronicles # 10

"Listen up, all of you," said Eagle. Buzz, Falcon, Hawk, and Owl were sitting in the salon of *Raptor* , facing him as he spoke.

"From what Falcon and I have seen at the Marina, the FBI is looking for us," continued Eagle.

Buzz, Falcon, Hawk, and Owl looked at each other but remained silent.

"What we need to do is take charge of the situation."

"How will we do that," said Hawk.

"By getting onto the *Lost & Found* and getting them to help us," said Eagle.

"How the fuck are we going to do that," said Owl.

"Tonight, we will sail the *Tayana* into the large gathering of sailboats in the bay, blending in with the rest. When Mr. Beaumont leaves in the morning to go shore to meet his FBI pal, we will very silently and quickly board the *Lost & Found* and take over."

"I love it," said Falcon, a huge grin on his face, thoughts of blood on his mind.

Chapter Forty

The next morning Yvonne and I were up at 8 and went to the salon.

"Hi, you two, about time you got up. Coffee is made. Join me on the fantail?"

"You bet, Cappy," said Yvonne.

"Mmm," I said.

"Gee, Boots, a hell of a greeting," said Cappy with a broad smile.

"I'm not awake yet. Coffee, Coffee."

"I'm getting it for you, Boots."

"Thanks, Vonnie. I'll need to be awake when I talk to Red, that's for sure."

"What do you think you'll do, Boots?" asked Cappy.

"I think it's up to how much Red can get the Coast Guard to help."

"You mean track the sub and the sailboat?"

"Exactly. I hope he has enough juice to get them to help."
"What kind of juice? I'm confuzzled," said Yvonne who just came out on the fantail with my coffee.

Cappy chuckled and said, "Yvonne, Juice is slang for having powerful friends who can make things happen."

"You Americans are bazarre." said, Yvonne.

Cappy chuckled again but said nothing.

I decided that 'bazarre' would be another of Yvonne's unusual word choices that I would hang on to.

"I've got to go meet Red. I want you two to be on high alert, ok?"

"Yes, sir, Cap'n." said, Cappy with a wink.

"Yes, sir, sir." said Yvonne with a big grin

I went down the ladder, got into the zodiac and started the motor with one good pull. The water in the bay was as smooth as glass and there was a gentle breeze on my face as I putted over to the beach near Bonnie's and tied up. I waved to Bonnie as I walked into the condo sales office.

"May I help you?" asked a beautiful young blonde woman in a casual pants suit with the name 'Sondra' embroidered over her left breast.

"Good morning, Sondra."

"Good morning, suh."

"Sondra, would you please look out the window in your back door. An FBI agent will be there and show you his badge."

"How do I know you are not going to rob me?"

"You can call over to Bonnie's and ask her or Denis if Boots, that's me, and Red, the FBI agent are trustworthy."

Sondra stared at me for a moment, smiled and said, "I think you'd not even say that if you were bad people. Wait, I'll go check."

I had trouble not staring at her cute figure as she went through the door to the back room of the office.

"Boots, I let him in. He would like you to go to the back and talk there."

"Thank you, Sondra. If by any chance anyone comes in here asking where I am, tell them I'm in the rest room. I'll hear them and deal with it."

I went to the back and closed the door. Red was sitting on a folding chair at a folding card table. There were empty food containers on the table.

"Hey, Boots. Good morning."

"Morning, Red. How are ya?"

"I'm worried, that's how I am."

"Do you have any ideas as to where to go from here?"

"I see two possibilities, Boots."

"Such as?"

"One, we wait until the sub and sailboat get underway and follow them to see what they are up to."

"Yes, and?" I asked.

"Two, we raid the *Raptor* now."

"What does your gut tell you to do, Red?"

"Tell the Coast Guard that we, the FBI, want them to put a 24/7 watch on the sub and the sailboat and immediately alert me when they start moving and keep us informed in play by play fashion."

"That would be my choice too. Can you let me know as it happens?"

"Of course, Boots, of course. See ya." Red looked out the windowed rear door and slipped out. I watched as he started up the path to the Tracy Way.

I opened the storeroom door a crack, looked in to make sure there were no visitors and went into the rental office.

"Sondra, did anyone come in or walk by while I was in the back?"

"No, suh. Not a soul"

"Thank you for helping us out.

"You are most welcome, suh," said, Sondra with a grin and a wink. "Any time."

I got the idea she was flirting with me and if I was not involved I would have asked her out, but visions of Yvonne flashed in my head. She was my one and only.

I walked out of the sales office and walked over to Bonnie's for a quick burger. I took a table under an umbrella and sat facing the beach. There was a nice off-shore breeze carrying the wonderful scent of bougainvillea. Denis served me in his friendly, efficient way and my burger was superb. My inner alarm bells were going off so I ate too fast, went to the zodiac and got on my way back to my boat and my gal. I always trusted my guts. This is one time that I wanted my gut feeling of danger to be wrong. *Be okay, Vonnie. Just be okay.*

Chapter Forty-One

There was a slight chop in the water as I steered the zodiac across the bay towards *Lost & Found*. My guts were screaming as I pulled up to the transom, got on the ladder and tied off to a cleat. "Yo, Cappy? Yvonne?" I heard no reply. I grabbed my pistol from under the dash and went into the salon, gun in my hand. The salon was empty. The boat 'felt' empty. I knew they were not on board but I checked any way. My heart was pounding with terror for my friend and for my lover.

I went back to the fantail. There was a small pool of blood on the cushion and even more on the deck. I almost missed it because my eyes seemed to be a bit blurred with tears but on the cushion I could make out 'Ik' traced in the blood. Nothing else, just 'Ik.' Ik is Dutch for 'I.' Why would Yvonne trace that unless... Duh, she was telling me *eye* as in eye of a raptor.

I took out my cell and dialed. As it was ringing I looked for the kittens and found them hiding under the kitchen sink, shaking. I was shaking as well. The boat was rocking a lot and from that and the smell in the air, I knew a storm was coming.

"Hi, Boots, what's up?"

"They took Cappy and Yvonne, Red. I need help and fast. There was blood on the fantail cushion and deck. Yvonne scrawled in Dutch to..."

There was movement behind me and a blinding light and then nothing.

Chapter Forty-Two

I awoke to an unfamiliar voice asking, "Yvonne scrawled in Dutch to let you know what, Mr. Beaumont?"

The back of my head felt like it was on fire and as big as a watermelon. I opened my eyes and through a curtain of red pain, saw that I was in the lounge of *Lost and Found.* The curtains were drawn so I couldn't tell if it was day or night. I could feel the gentle motion of the waves underneath the boat and knew we were underway. I tried to push back the pain so I could stay alert.

"I ask you again, Mr. Beaumont, Yvonne scrawled in Dutch to let you know what?" He screamed this time, "What?"

"To let me know she loved me," I said.

I looked up and saw him for the first time. He was standing in front of me. He was tall, tanned, wearing a freshly pressed white trousers and a light blue Guayabera shirt. His eyes were small and beady, lips drawn back in a scowl. There was a tattoo of a raptors eye on the side of his neck.

"That's what she scrawled," I continued.

"Why didn't I see the message in Dutch words?" said, Eagle.

"I put my hands in the blood and smeared it when I fell against the cushion as a wave moved the boat under me. Where is she?"

I didn't see his fist until the last second and then it was too late to move my head. I saw stars, the sun as well. Only when the stars faded did I realize I was standing with my back to the galley pass-through counter facing the lounge. I was tied with my hands behind my back. It seemed to be electrical cord and I could not figure out what it was secured to.

"Where is she?" I demanded again.

"She is with your friend who won't give me his name. Or should I say has not *yet* given me his name. Don't worry, they are both fine for now."

"Who are you?"

"You may call me Eagle, Mr. Beaumont. And you can stop struggling. You can't get loose."

"Where are you taking us?"

"You are going to take us all for a sail, Mr. Beaumont. You will call your friends at the FBI and tell them you've decided to sail to St. Martin. Yvonne wants to go to the Dutch side of the island and explore. We'll have a jolly cruise. Then you'll decide to sell this boat to some people I know who will meet us there."

"I'm not doing to do that, Eagle. No way."

"I think you will, Mr. Beaumont. I think you will beg me to let you do exactly that… "

Chapter Forty-Three

Eagle gave me a wink and yelled, "Falcon, bring the girl up here."

I strained against the rope as I looked at the different entrances to the salon, waiting for Yvonne to appear. Eagle sat down on one of the salon chairs. He seemed to be as tense as a coiled spring.

Yvonne stumbled into the room from the aft cabin stairway, hands tied behind her back with electrical wire, being pushed by a man with a hooked nose, black eyes, unruly black hair, barefoot and dressed in black t-shirt and jeans. He had that same tattoo of a raptor's eye on the side of his neck. He had a knife pressed against her cheek.

"Mr. Beaumont, say hello to Falcon."

"Leave her alone, you bastards."

"Mr. Beaumont, such language. Shame on you."

"Leave her alone, she has nothing to do with any of this."

"Oh but she does, Mr. Beaumont. How about our little voyage to St. Martin? Her life depends on it."

"Fuck you."

The man called Falcon pressed the knife into her cheek until it drew a drop of blood. Yvonne flinched but doesn't make a sound.

"Enough Falcon."

"Mr. Beaumont, do you get the point?" asked Eagle with a laugh. "She sure did."

"Yeah, I got it."

Falcon pulled Yvonne over to the couch and pushed her down on her face, tying her off to one of the legs of the coffee table. She squirmed around so that she was on her side, facing me.

"Leave her alone. I'll do what you want. Where is Cappy?" I was thinking as fast as I could in order to gain some time.

"He is below."

"I want to see that him." I was thinking as fast as I could

"No, I don't want the three of you together."

"He is my therapist so I need him in the room to keep me from losing my cool."

"Good God. One of those American losers who needs his own shrink. Okay, okay. Falcon, have Buzz bring the therapist up here."

Falcon went below and as Eagle watched him, I looked at Yvonne and smiled. She looked at me and smiled. I smiled back and winked.

Within less than a minute, Cappy was led through the passageway from the aft cabin stairway by a stunning woman, dressed all in white, wearing sandals. Falcon brought up the rear. Cappy was also bound by electrical wire. He had a black eye, a bit of blood on his forehead leaking from a small loose flap of skin. He was pushed down on the other end of the couch and tied to the opposite end of the table from Yvonne. Cappy looked at Falcon, then at me, expressionless.

"Falcon, go to the cockpit and keep a look out. Mr. Beaumont say hello to Buzzard, called Buzz."

"Hello, Buzzard."

"Hello Mr. Beaumont," she said.

She looked me directly in the eye and turned away very quickly. It puzzled me. I made a mental note to watch her carefully. I could tell by Cappy's face that he noticed it as well.

The sound of seagulls searching for lunch penetrated the think silence of my boat. You could cut the tension with a knife.

"So, Mr. Beaumont, what will it be? Eh?"

Eagle looked at me, then pointed at Cappy and Yvonne with his fingers shaped like a gun and simulated pulling a trigger with his thumb.

Who says, "Eh" I asked myself. Canadians, that's who. I filed that info with Buzzards eye movements.

Yvonne and Cappy both winced. I felt terror and rage. Out loud in my head, I told myself to stay calm and alert.

"Ok, Mr. Eagle, I'll do what you wish. Who will be at the helm?"

"You and I will be at the helm, Buzz will stay in the salon to guard your friends. I am going to untie you. One move, one tiny mistake and your friends will become very unhappy indeed. Let's go up to the helm now."

He pulled a small revolver from his pocket and waved it in my direction with one hand as he untied my hands with his other one. He motioned for me to go past him. We went aft and up the passageway to the helm with me in the lead. I tried to make contact with Cappy and Yvonne before I went up but could not. Falcon was at the wheel and I realized that we were barely making way, perhaps 2 knots per hour. From the trip in, I recognized that we had just left Cowpet Bay, entered St. James Bay and turned to starboard on a southerly heading.

"Falcon, I don't think Mr. Beaumont will give us any problems so check on the sub, make sure it's riding well below the surface. In another few minutes or so, we slow to a crawl, you'll get in the sub and go back to base and stay with Owl while Hawk takes the Tayana to the buyer on Antigua. We'll continue south until we are past Great St. James Island, then southeast to St. Kitts."

"Yvonne will be very disappointed that we are not going to St. Martin."

"That's such a shame. Now, Mr. Beaumont, get on the phone to the FBI and tell them what I told you to say. One wrong word and your friends will pay dearly."

Chapter Forty-Four

The phone rang six times and I was about to give up when it was answered. Falcon was at the helm. Both he and Eagle were watching me closely. Eagle always had his gun in hand.

"Hello? Baron here. Who's calling?"

"Boots Beaumont."

"Hello, Mr. Beaumont, Are you ok? You sound funny."

"I'm fine, Mr. Baron. It's just the cell service being a bit fuzzy. I just wanted to let you know that we've decided to sail to St. Martin. Yvonne wants to go to the Dutch side of the island and explore. Cappy is with us and we'll just take our time, no rush."

"I'm glad all is well. Have a great time."

"Thanks, Mr. Baron. Bye."

"Well done, Mr. Beaumont. Well done indeed."

"Falcon, I'll take the helm. We'll slow to a crawl, enough time for you to get in and get moving. You can go to the sub now," said, Eagle and pulled the throttle back as far as it would go.

"Roger, Eagle," said Falcon and went through the aft cabin door.

We were rocking gently in the swells, just barely making way. I heard a splash then moments later two knocks on the hull.

"He's in the sub now so let's continue, shall we," said Eagle as he pushed the throttle forward. We picked up enough speed to stop the rocking, my guess was about six knots.

"We are past Dog Island so, I'll put us on auto-pilot heading of 120, then we can go below. Is that all right with you, Mr. Beaumont?" He adjusted our heading and put the autopilot on.

"Yes, of course, Eagle. Anything you say." I was watching him very carefully, looking for any opening.

Eagle smiled and gave me a poke in the kidney with the gun. "Move." He smiled again as I walked past him and went below.

"Buzz, would you make us all some lunch? I don't want to keep our guests hungry while we are on our way to St. Kitts. Perhaps take the young lady with you? She won't give you any trouble, not if she knows what's good for her."

Buzzard went over to Yvonne and untied her from the table and pulled her across the salon to the galley. Yvonne kept her head down and did not look at me or Buzzard. Cappy stared after them.

"Eagle, can I ask a question?"

"Can't stop you now, can I, eh? What is it?"

"What happens when we get to St. Kitts?

"Well now. That sort of depends. I figure I need you and Cappy here to help run the boat for the next 7 days until we get there. Once we arrive, the buyers will look over this boat and the young lady. They may want to give us a bonus for her. Me thinks you two men will not be of further use to us. The buyers will take charge of the rest." Eagle smirked and turned away.

"Eagle, may I ask another?"

"Yes, what is it this time?"

"May I use the head?"

Chapter Forty-Five

"You can use the head, Mr. Beaumont but just remember what happens if you get cute."

"Yes, I know." I went forward and down to my office and closed the cabin door.

"Leave that door open. I want to hear you, Mr. Beaumont."

I opened the door, used the toilet and turned on the water in the sink. I wanted a minute to make sure my pistol was still in its hiding place behind the mirror and it was. The mirror was on a hinge with the latch mechanism hidden under the sink behind the pipes. Cappy, handy with his hands, had built this hiding place long ago. I closed the mirror, leaving the gun behind for the time being. Eagle and Buzzard both had guns so I needed to bide my time. My eyes and ears needed to be on super alert.

"What is taking so long, Mr. Beaumont?"

"Coming, coming, I was washing the grease off of my hands."

I turned off the water and went back to the galley. Buzzard and Yvonne had made sandwiches and set them on the table in front of the couch. Cappy was sitting up, hands free but one leg tied to the aft table leg. Yvonne was sitting next to Cappy. I sat across from Yvonne. Eagle sat on my right and Buzzard was on his right. I gave Cappy a quick look and a very slight nod. I know that he knew I had found the pistol in the head.

We ate quietly, Eagle and Buzzard keeping a close eye on the three of us. Not that we could really do anything with Cappy and Yvonne having one leg tied to the table.

"Eagle?"

"Yes, what do you want?" Eagle said this with almost a snarl, as opposed to his almost too polite language."

"Aren't you worried about us getting hit by another boat or going a ground on a hidden reef?"

"Don't you trust your auto-pilot?"

"Well yes, but they are not infallible? Can't one or all of us be up in the bridge or the outdoor cockpit?"

"I think all or nothing, so, let the two women clean up from lunch and we'll go to the outdoor helm," said Eagle in his more normal calm voice. . Buzzard gave him a funny look.

"Why should we have to clean up? You ate too," said Buzzard.

Eagle's free hand moved like lightening, smacking Buzzard across the face. It was so fast she didn't have time to duck.

In an instant, Buzzard's face went from pain to showing nothing.

"Like I said, you women clean up. And untie Cappy so he can join Mr. Beaumont and me at the helm. We wouldn't want him to be lonely down here."

Buzzard turned away and untied Cappy and Yvonne. Yvonne and Cappy both looked at me. Yvonne turned away, her fear was written all over her face. Cappy walked over to Eagle and me, expressionless. Buzzard started cleaning up with Yvonne helping at her side.

I went up to the steps to the bridge with Cappy… Eagle close behind. The cabin was filled with sunlight, the sea calm. Cappy sat on the stern cushion, and sat back with his eyes closed. Eagle quickly went to him and tied his left arm to one of the cleats. Cappy seemed totally unaware. I quickly checked the autopilot and said, "Eagle, as long as we have to wait for the women, why are you doing this?"

"Why wouldn't I, Mr. Beaumont, why wouldn't I?"

"I'm more interested in why you do."

"I could care less, Mr. Beaumont."

"Why not call me Boots?" I said. I heard the deep sound of a freighter passing in the distance.

"That would imply friendship, that's why and we will not know each other long enough for that to occur."

A shiver went down my spine. I tried not to show it when I responded. "Then why not share your reason?"

"What is this, a talk show?" said, Eagle.

"Did I make you angry?" I had a germ of an idea and wanted to push a bit."

"You? Make *me* angry? Ha."

I was not convinced. His voice gave him away. "Yes, *you*, you sound angry."

"Well, I'm not so let's change the subject." Eagle sounded even more angry.

I knew he was getting distracted. If only I could get him talking and distracted when Yvonne was up here. If I could arrange to get to the head, then get Cappy untied as well… There would be a chance… Buzzard's reaction time would be the key.

Chapter Forty-Six

"What the fuck is taking those women so long to clean up down there?" said Eagle loudly.

It was beginning to rain and we were gliding into a gray mist. I could feel the boat responding to a light chop in the sea.

"I need to use the head, Eagle. You have Cappy for insurance. Can I go down to the head and tell Buzzard you are waiting for her in the cockpit?"

"Yeah, go do it," snarled Eagle, seated at the helm.

He was looking forward so I snuck a glance at Cappy who gave a slight nod.

I went below and saw Buzzard and Yvonne in the galley. It looked like they were talking. I said, "Eagle told me it was ok to use the head."

Buzzard nodded and kept talking to Yvonne as I went forward and down the few steps to my office and head. I went in, closed and locked the door and reached beneath the sink for the latch to let the mirror swing open. I put my hand in, grabbed my gun and put it inside the pocket of my shorts. I latched the mirror, flushed the toilet and went out of the head. I went up the steps to the salon, my heart pounding.

Yvonne and Buzzard were still talking as I walked across the salon. I heard a yell from above, "Hey Buzz, what the fuck is taking so long? Get your ass up here with the bitch, ok?"

Buzzard's eyes narrowed then got wide as she smiled and took out her gun, pointing it at the deck. She looked at me and whispered. "I've had enough of his shit. I'm with you. Hurry before I chicken out." She motioned with her head for Yvonne to stay. Yvonne smiled at me, fear and hope in her eyes. I smiled back and mouthed, "I love you."

I could not believe what I heard Buzzard say. I looked at her, nodded, took out my gun and held it behind my back. We headed up the steps, Buzzard first, gun out, pointing back at me.

"Eagle, Beaumont was acting up," said Buzzard.

"Do you have him under control, Buzz?" said Eagle, turning.

"Yes, and now I have you under control," replied Buzzard as she turned the gun to point at Eagle. "Do not move."

"Have you lost your mind, Buzz?" said Eagle.

"No, Eagle, I just got it back. Don't you move."

"You fucking bitch." said Eagle, glaring at her and pointing his gun at her.

I was spellbound, too frightened to move a muscle. I was frozen in time, smelling the salt air, feeling the gentle motion of the swells under the boat and hearing the lapping of the water against the hull.

I saw everything in slow motion. Buzzard fired and Eagle fired as he fell. Buzzard fired again. I heard a sound behind me and turning, saw Yvonne fall to the deck, red spreading on her blouse.

I rushed to her and held her in my arms. She spoke softly and said, "Boots?"

"Yes, lieve?" I said, tears streaming down my face

"Don't leave me. Please?" she said, looking in my eyes.

"I won't leave you, Vonnie," I said stifling the sobs.

"Do you prom…"

And she was still. "Come back lieve Vonnie. Come back and I'll go out and I'll buy you the moon," I whispered in her ear. "Fuck," I said out loud and put my head in my hands, unaware that wetness I felt was tears falling from Cappy's eyes as he knelt beside me with his hand on my shoulder.

Chapter Forty-Seven

Cappy led me to the salon where Buzzard was sitting on the sofa with a glass of wine in her hand. I sat on the sofa and Cappy pulled over one of the salon chairs.

"This is all I have of her, Cappy. This is all I have of my Vonnie," I said, showing him the blood on my hands. Blood that came from my shirt where her blood had flowed when I held her in my arms. "It's my fucking fault. It's my fucking fault.. It's as if my lights have gone out. I love her so much and we had such a short time together. Fucking son of a bitch." I got up and walked around the salon, shaking my fist. "I am so angry. I hurt so badly. I want her back, damn it all. I want her back."

I felt Cappy pull me back to the sofa. He gave me a hug and a glass of wine.

Through all of this, Buzzard was silent, head bowed, tears running down her cheeks.

"No, Mr. Beaumont, it's my fault, not yours. I should never ever have done what I did. I thought we were going to steal boats, not kill people. I will surely go to hell for what I did." She started to shake, her body wracked with sobs.

I saw Cappy go over and sit beside her. "What did you do, exactly?" he said quietly.

She spoke softly, so softly I could hardly hear her.

"I drove the sub while Falcon went aboard boats in the middle of the night and killed the owners so we could steal it. I didn't sign up for it but once it started, I had no way out." She started to sob again, tears flowing like little streams coming down a mountainside.

"How did you get started, Buzzard? And what is your real name?"

She sniffed and said, "My name is Cathy Parsley. I was born in Russia, was placed in an orphanage, adopted by Americans and grew up in Scranton. I was always fascinated by raptors and saw a Facebook group for raptor lovers. I met the others on that group's page."

She sighed and said, "There's more. I was a stripper in a fancy bar. I never did more than that, I mean only that I wouldn't do anything with anyone outside the bar, but I'm still ashamed of it," and she lowered her head.

It occurred to me that the autopilot was still pointing us towards St. Kitts. I left them talking and went up to the bridge. I reset our course to northwest towards St. Thomas. I dragged Eagle's body to the stern rail. I was going to give him to the fish for lunch but first I needed to talk to Red. I took out my cellphone and called.

"FBI field office."

"Red Baron please, Boots Beaumont calling," I said.

"This is Red Baron. Boots, what's going on?"

"Yvonne is dead, Red." I started to sob. I hadn't said the words out loud and it hit me like a ton of bricks.

"Boots, are you ok? Is Cappy ok? What happened?" asked Red rapidly.

"I'll tell you later but for now, Falcon left in the sub about an hour ago, heading back to *Raptor*'s mooring in Cowpet bay. Supposedly Owl and

Hawk are there as well. Please get the Coast Guard to pick him up. Eagle is dead but none of those three know that."

"Will do, Boots. Where are you now?"

"Heading northwest, about 100 miles southeast of Great St. James Island.

"Call me when you are an hour out and I'll have a Coast Guard cutter escort you to your mooring."

"Roger and out," I said.

I went below. Cappy & Buzzard were still talking in low voices on the couch. I took the few steps down to my stateroom and saw Pietje and Stafje sitting on the bed, staring at me expectantly, tails waving, purring loudly. I hugged them both and said quietly, "She won't be back. Our Vonnie won't be back."

Chapter Forty-Eight

I heard a noise, a roar, coming closer. I ran topside and saw a jetliner descending rapidly, flames shooting out of the left engine. I saw bodies falling in flames from one of the windows. One of them was a flight attendant. I could tell it was Yvonne, screaming, "Boots, help me. Please help me." I jumped in the water and started to swim to her, the plane heading for me, for her. Flames everywhere.

I screamed, "I'm coming, Yvonne, I'm coming. Hang on, lieve, hang on. Don't let go, Don't die, don't die, Don't Donnnnnnnn."

I opened my eyes and looked around. I was sitting up in bed, covered in sweat, heart racing.

It took me a few minutes to realize that it was only a dream but the reality was, my Vonnie was dead. Gone forever. I met her when her plane crashed in the sea a few years ago… crashed because a mad man had sabotaged it. Now she was taken from me because another mad man had shot her.

I sobbed once, got up and hopped into the shower. After a good hot scrub, I got out and put on a pair of cut-offs and went up to the salon. There was coffee but no people so I went to the cockpit. Cappy and Buzz were there drinking coffee.

"Morning Boots," said Cappy.

"Morning, Cap, morning Buzz," I said.

"Good morning, Mr. Beaumont," said Buzzard without looking at me. She was wearing blue shorts and white T-shirt and Cappy was wearing cut-offs.

I felt the boat rocking gently and heard the sound of the waves slapping against the hull.

I sipped my coffee and looked up at the sky.

"I think a storm is on the way, you two. It could get rough."

"Gee thanks, Boots," said Cappy.

"You are most welcome, Cap. I think that…"

My cell phone rang and I saw it was Red calling.

"Yo, Red. What's up?"

"Not good, Boots, not good at all."

"What do you mean, Red?"

"The Coast Guard found the sub, empty, tied up at *Raptor*. Raptor is empty. They searched the entire boat and there is no one on board. Falcon, Hawk and Owl are missing."

"Good God, Red. Does the Coast Guard have any idea at all where they might be?"

"No, Boots. By the time they got to the boat it was too late. They are going through *Raptor*, inch by inch looking for clues but so far nothing. I think you need to be very careful.

"I sure will. Thanks, Red."

"Keep me posted, pal," said Red and hung up.

"Cappy, Buzz, we have a problem."

"The storm?"

"Worse than that, much worse."

Chapter Forty-Nine

"Boots, what did Red say? You've got me worried," said Cappy.

"Hawk, Owl and Falcon were not on the *Raptor*. They put out a BOLO but so far nothing."

"What's a BOLO?" asked Buzzard.

"It means, be on the lookout for, Buzz," said Cappy.

"We've had a rough time so I think that we need to get a good rest so that we can be on the lookout too," I said. "Meanwhile one of us needs to be at the helm. The autopilot can only do so much."

"Buzz, can we trust you?" I said.

"Yes, Mr. Boots, you can," she said, looking at me directly for the first time.

"Good. You can have the forward cabin opposite Cappy. Get a good rest. Cappy will show you the way. I'll be in my stateroom aft if you need me. Cappy, take the 1st watch please."

Buzz nodded. Cappy said, "Aye aye, skipper," and gave me a salute and headed forward followed by Buzzard.

I was about to go to my cabin when Cappy came back.

"She's sacked out now, Boots. Got a minute?" said Cappy.

"Sure, Cap. What's up?" I said.

"Boots, I'm just so angry at what happened to Buzz. She was two years old, living in an orphanage in Russia. She was brought to the U.S. and adopted by a family in Scranton. They knew no Russian and

Buzz knew no English. She was terrified and spoke to her new parents in the little bit of Russian she was able to speak. They got enraged at her and beat her. She stopped talking so they beat her even more. As she learned English she started to say how sad she was that she lost her family, country and heritage. They beat her more. She ran away from her home, not too far and wound up at the strip club in her home town of Scranton. That she survived her childhood without becoming a psychopath is an amazing testament to the good genes she got from her natural family. I just feel for her, Boot," said Cappy, wiping a tear from his left eye with the back of his palm.

I gave him a hugs and said, "I understand, old friend."

"Thanks, Boots," said, Cappy and turned to go up to the helm

I went aft and down the few steps to my stateroom. I could feel the boat change course a bit, and smell the fresh breeze from the cross ventilation through the portholes. I lay down for a nap.

I heard a scream. "Yvonne?" I yelled, "Are you ok?" I heard the scream again. I realized that I had been dreaming but the screams were real. I shook my head and started to sit up.

"Do not move, Mr. Beaumont. Be very still," said a voice.

I opened my eyes and saw an unfamiliar face pointing a gun at me. "Who the fuck are you? And what are you doing on my boat?" I said as I stared to sit up.

I was smashed across the side of my head and a searing pain traveled down my body. "You do not need to use profanity, Mr. Beaumont. My name is Hawk and you have caused me and my companions a lot of grief."

"Where are Cappy and Buzz?" I said.

"They are tied up at the moment," said Hawk.

"Why are you here? What the fuck a…"

I didn't finish the sentence. He whacked me on the side of the head so fast I didn't see his hand move.

"I told you, no profanity. I meant it. Try me again, Mr. Beaumont. Just one more time," Hawk said with fire in his eyes.

"And, since you asked, we are here to continue our mission. You and your friends will be disposed of once we figure out how to get the Coast Guard off our backs. Now, get up and walk quietly with me to the salon," Hawk said as he yanked me to my feet. "My gun not only hits but shoots bullets as well."

I saw Cappy, bleeding from his forehead, slumped on the starboard sofa. Buzzard was on the floor lying next to Cappy's feet, moaning softly, blood oozing from her nose. Two men, with twisted smiles on their faces, were standing near the galley pass-through, watching them.

"Meet the Owl and the Falcon, Mr. Beaumont. The three of us are to be trite, your worst nightmare come true," said Hawk.

Chapter Fifty

I looked at the three of them standing together by the galley pass-through, looking quite proud of themselves. I needed some time to think and my brain was still a bit confuzzled from being hit with Hawk's gun.

"How did you get here, Mr. Hawk?" I said.

"Well, why not tell you," said, Hawk. "We heard the alert go out on *Raptor's* scanner. Falcon and I get on the sub to go boat hunting and lo and behold just as we were about to cast off from *Raptor*, a big old Grand Banks motor-cruiser comes burbling into the cove not twenty feet away, so Owl, standing on *Raptor* puts on his best smile and waves at the couple on the deck of the cruiser. They wave back. The guy at the helm stops the boat and yells, 'Hey, a sub, can we see it?' Owl yells, 'Sure. What's your name.' By God, the guy says, 'I'm Marcus and my wife is Marijke' and turns his boat towards us. The guy throws Falcon here a rope to tie up. Falcon ties it to one of the sub's deck cleats. I jump on board the cruiser and tell the guy to take a look. Falcon holds his hand out. The guy takes it and hops on the sub and in an instant Falcon says, 'Nice to meet you, Marcus, welcome aboard' and puts a knife in his belly. His wife gets part of a scream out and I grab her, putting one hand over her mouth. I tell her to not make a sound or I'll kill her. She nods her head and smiles. I smile back, say 'Good Marijke,' and put a knife in her back before she can blink. Falcon and Owl helped me get the bodies of the guy and the woman on to *Raptor* and below decks. Falcon cuts them into pieces with the Sawzall and then puts them into that huge freezer that Eagle had installed."

"So how did you find us?" I asked. I knew I needed to keep him talking. I needed time. I wasn't sure how I would use it but I sure needed it. I saw Cappy's eyes open slightly. Buzzard was not moving. The boat was rocking in the waves and I could smell the salt. I heard a seagull's call. What I wanted to hear was the sounds of being rescued. I'm used to not getting what I want.

"Since you asked, Mr. Beaumont, I'll tell you. We three got on the motor-cruiser with as much of the stashed money that we could find. Owl has a hand held GPS and used it to find Eagle's cell phone's GPS signal. We found your boat, tied up near the bow and came aboard while you were all sacked out and took over. And speaking of over, we threw Eagle's body over… over to the sharks," said Hawk giggling. His eyes were reflecting rays of light from the water that seemed to match his giggling.

"Thanks for the memory, Mr. Hawks. I'm curious. How come Mr. Owl and Mr. Falcon haven't said a word? Are they silent for a reason?" I said.

"They are just biding their time, Mr. Beaumont. Falcon, back to the bridge, please. Owl, keep an eye on these two wounded ducks. You and Falcon can have them soon enough."

Falcon left the salon without a sound. Owl grinned and moved across the salon and sat on one of the swivel chairs facing Cappy and Buzzard. He turned to Hawk and said, "Aye Aye." He turned back and smiled at Cappy and Buzzard. I think he winked at them but I not sure.

Out of the corner of my eye I caught a glimpse of movement past one of the portside salon windows behind Owl. I saw Cappy's eyes move slightly and am sure he saw the movement as well and was on the alert. I took stock. Hawk had a gun. I'd seen it. Owl and Falcon were wearing cut-offs and I'd seen no signs of a gun on either of them. I knew from what Hawk had said that Falcon had a knife. I was hoping I was right in thinking that Owl was unarmed.

I heard a noise from above decks that sounded like a thousand eagles diving for salmon at the same time.

Chapter Fifty-One

Hawk turned and started towards the passage to the helm. I reacted without thought, my training in the military taking over. I launched myself at him, my focus on the gun in his left hand. We both fell to the deck. I had his gun hand in both mine so he hit me on top of my head with the fist of his other hand. It hurt like hell but I ignored it as best as I could and did the only thing I could think of.. I bit the wrist of his gun hand. He yelled and struggled but my hands were stronger than his so he had to let the gun drop. He grabbed me around the neck with both his hands and squeezed.

My world started to go dark when I heard a sound like a balloon suddenly releasing its' air, and I felt his hands just drop off. He went limp and dropped on the steps. I looked up and saw a very disheveled woman, perhaps thirty, brunette hair across her dirt smeared forehead, dressed in stained jeans and a torn T-shirt. She was breathing very hard, crying, blood dripping from a cut on her cheek and from the knife she held in her right hand. Her T-shirt had an Avis logo with the words, Wij proberen steeds meer in a Dutch script.

'He is dead? Dat monster is dead?" she said in a familiar accent.

"Yes, he is. Who are you? And are you ok?" I said as I struggled to stand up. I wondered who she was but more to the point, where did she come from. She seemed to have appeared by magic.

I looked behind me. Cappy had picked up a table lamp and conked Owl on the head then trussed him with the lamp cord. Buzz was sitting on the sofa holding her head but smiling. Cappy was also on the sofa, smiling. Both were looking at the woman who dropped in and saved our lives. I was breathing hard, excited and relieved and my adrenalin was flowing like Niagara Falls.

"My name Helena, what your name?" she said in a trembling voice. Her eyes were wide open and her face was pale. She appeared dazed.

"I'm Boots and Cappy and Buzz are on the couch. Where did you come from? How did you get here, Helena? I'm baffled."

She took a deep breath and said, "I was in de galley of a motorboat with friends of mine from Netherlands when I heard a yelling und looked up und saw free people with guns come in from da outside to de salon and dey murders my friends. Dey couldn't see me so I ducked into de motor place und stayed dere until it seemed safe for me to come out. It was very Greecy in der between dos motors. I tink I fallen asleep for a time. I came out und saw dat we were tied up to this boat und saw det monster fellow at de helm. I snucked up on him and stabbed him in de back from behind. Den, I saw another one of dem monsters chocking you so I fixed him gud."

"I, I don't know what to say except thank you, Helena. Thank you. Are you ok?"

"I tink so. I know I cuts myself a bit squeezing between de motors but I tink I am ok. But I am very um, filth. Pardon my English. I am learning fast as I can. Can I get to clean up und some closes to wear too?" Helena asked.

"Sure, come with me, and your English is just fine," said Buzz and then led Helena to the forward stateroom. Helena left behind a trace of lilac in the air.

"Cappy, are you ok?" I said

"Yes, Boots. Drained but ok. What do we do with this chap?" Cappy said, looking at the trussed up Owl.

"We keep him on ice until we get back to St. Thomas. As to Hawk and Falcon, didn't they jump overboard when Helena showed up with her knife? Didn't I just hear them?"

"You know, Boots, I think they did jump overboard. Thanks for reminding me."

"You're welcome, my friend. In the meantime, we have a trilemma," I said.

" Trilemma?"

"Yes, Trilemma, Cap. Three problems at the same time."

"What three, Boots?"

"We have to convince Owl that he remembers the other two jumping overboard before we hand him over to the FBI. We have to decide what to do with Buzzard and finally, what do we do with Helena?"

"Well, I can tell you one thing, Boots. Listening to her accent, Helena is from Holland and Dutch women seem to be your specialty."

"Yes, they sure are, Cap," I said as I shed a tear or two or three. *God I missed my Vonnie.*

Chapter Fifty-Two

"Mr. Beaumont?" said Buzzard in a trembling voice as she came up from the passageway from the stateroom below. She was dressed in clean cut-offs, a batik blouse and sneakers.

"Yes, Buzz? And please call me Boots."

"What are you going to do with me?" she said.

"What do you *think* we should do with you, Buzz?" asked Cappy.

"I've been thinking about it myself. I know I did wrong things. I know I won't do them again. I want to be punished but I don't know what's right," said Buzzard.

"I was going to say one thing but hearing you say what you just said, I've changed my mind. I leave it up to Cappy."

"Buzz, the jails on Eleuthera or here in St. Thomas are not fit for anyone. If you were facing charges in the states, I'd suggest you throw yourself on the mercy of the courts. But here in the Caribbean, you would be punished unfairly. And you sound very sincere so, I've changed my mind too, Buzz. I think if you agree to see a therapist friend of mine, and work on yourself, that will be all that is necessary," said Cappy.

Buzzard was crying and through her tears managed to say, "Yes, thank you, yes I will see a therapist."

"Now we're back to a dilemma," I said, "Owl and Helena."

"Boots, leave Owl to me. I know how to take care of the problem. Helena I leave to you, and your knowledge of Dutch women."

"Thanks, pal," I said.

"Buzz, would you go below and make sure that Helena's ok?" I said.

"Sure, Boots," said, Buzz.

"Cappy, how about we let Helena sail back to St. Thomas with us and decide then?" I said.

"Fine with me. I'll see to Owl now," said Cappy.

Cappy got Owl un-trussed enough to stand and took him to the passageway that led up to the deck. Cappy looked over his shoulder and winked at me as he went up the stairs.

I was alone with and my heart-wrenching aching for Yvonne.

Chapter Fifty-Three

We were back in Cowpet Bay with *Lost and Found* at anchor.

Denis had just brought our meals to the table. There was a fresh, fragrant breeze from the west. The iguanas were having an early siesta since we were the only ones having a late lunch.

Cappy, Buzz, Helena and I were sitting at Bonnies having lunch.

"Owl was very docile wasn't he?" I said.

"Well, that makes sense considering if he keeps his mouth shut he'll not face murder charges," said, Cappy.

"He was always the quiet one when we had meetings," said Buzz, "of all of them, he was the only one I liked."

"Well, he'll have lots of quiet time for a long time," said Cappy.

"Tomorrow we will set sail for our home in Eleuthera. Buzz and Helena, you are free to sail with us or stay here on St. Thomas. It's up to you," I said.

"I want to go to Eleuthera and see your therapist friend, Boots," said, Buzz, and took a bite of her salad and a sip of her Amstel.

"Dat's for me the same, Boots," said, Helena and took a bite of her hamburger and a sip of her Amstel.

"Cappy said, "So what else is new?" and took a chunk of his salmonburger and a sip of his Amstel.

I dipped a piece of crab leg into butter, ate it, took a gulp of my Amstel and said, "Cappy, there is something I never told you…"

www.ingramcontent.com/pod-product-compliance
Lightning Source LLC
Chambersburg PA
CBHW060144130626
46556CB00006B/2480